Sherlock Holmes and the Angels of Vengeance

By Ray Crew

Paperback ISBN 978-1-80424-765-5
ePub ISBN 978-1-80424-766-2
PDF ISBN 978-1-80424-767-9

Published by MX Publishing
335 Princess Park Manor, Royal Drive,
London, N11 3GX
www.mxpublishing.com

Cover by Mike Fox

Author's Note

I came late to an appreciation of the characters created by Sir Arthur Conan Doyle. For most of my life my understanding of them was limited to pop culture cliché's. Then, through a series of serendipitous accidents I found myself cast as Holmes in an original stage play that took place over three days as part of a Sherlock Holmes weekend festival. I found I rather enjoyed the role and apparently the audience and producers enjoyed me in it because I went on to play the great consulting detective in original works written for that festival for the next ten years. I'm much more a writer than I am an actor so, after a while it was only natural that I would try my hand at an original Holmes tale. Combining my new appreciation of Holmes, Watson, Mrs. Hudson, Professor Moriarty et al. with my love of historical fiction, the stage play "Sherlock Holmes and the Avenging Angels" was born. It had a long and successful run in 2018. When it closed, I moved on to other projects and left the world of 221B, Baker Street behind. Then, in 2024 thanks to another series of serendipitous accidents, I met Gail Wagner, a theatrical producer, fellow film maker and master costumer. In the course of a Sunday afternoon conversation about a completely different topic the idea of turning my play into a film came up. Gail convinced me it could be done and thanks to her belief, encouragement and hard work as my executive producer, "Sherlock Holmes and the Angels of Vengeance" became a reality.

I will be eternally grateful to her and each member of the cast and crew who worked through a long, cold winter of location shooting to bring this story to the screen.

Ray Crew

Sherlock Holmes, Dr. John Watson, Mrs. Hudson, Irene Adler and Professor James Moriarty are characters created by Sir Arthur Conan Doyle. Loveday Brooke is a character created by Catherine Louisa Pirkis.

Anna Surratt Tonry, Thomas Boston Corbett, Susan Rebecca Corbett, John Wilkes Booth and Emma Goldman are based on real people. Everyone else is a product of the author's imagination.

Some of the events in this story actually happened. The rest could have.

The Characters *(In order of appearance)*

Irene – An American tourist and Arthur Conan Doyle aficionado – Kim Taylor

Mary – An American tourist and friend of Irene – Lezlie Eustis

Ellen – An American tourist and friend of Irene – Janice Bouchard-Hall

Sherlock Holmes – The famous consulting detective – Dave Baumberger

John Watson – Physician and associate of Sherlock Holmes – Tony Gerdes

Drusilla – A member of Reverend Thatcher's flock – Ruth Brittain

Flora – A member of Reverend Thatcher's flock – Mallory Vogl

Nigel – A member of Reverend Thatcher's flock – Barry Schechter

Bert – A member of Reverend Thatcher's flock – Len Hedges-Goettl

Thomas Boston Corbett aka Richard Thatcher – An American Preacher – Patrick Mulvaney

3

Madeline Hughes – A follower of Boston Corbett who is more than she appears – Erica Sefton

Mrs. Hudson – Holmes and Watson's landlady at 221B Baker Street – Gail Wagner

Anna Surratt Tonry – Daughter of Mary Surratt – Jill Liberaski

The Repent Woman – A street prophet – Gina Olkowski

Loveday Brooke – A young lady seeking employment with Ebenezer Dyer – Arianna Fox

Irene Adler – A former opera singer, actress, and adventuress – Cat Baker

Emma Goldman – The high priestess of anarchy – Luisa Forger

James Moriarty – International criminal mastermind – Chuck Rafftery

Bunny Blackstone – An Irish prison guard who talks with his fists – Steven Dow

A residential London street. Three women, Irene, Ellen and Mary, are consulting a tour guidebook and looking at the addresses on the houses they pass.

The Present

IRENE – Two fifteen….two seventeen…two nineteen. *(She looks up)* That's it.

ELLEN – Two twenty one B

MARY – This is where they lived then?

ELLEN – In the stories…yes

IRENE – *(Mesmerized)* And what stories they are

MARY – But they *are* just stories…right?

ELLEN – Yes

MARY – They weren't real people?

ELLEN – You never read Arthur Conan Doyle?

MARY – Who?

ELLEN – Never mind

IRENE – My mother read them to me

MARY – Like bedtime stories?

IRENE – Yes

ELLEN – That explains a lot

IRENE – Some stories she read…some stories she just told me

ELLEN – She had them memorized?

IRENE – No

MARY – She made them up?

IRENE – No…my grandmother told them to her…and my great grandmother told them to my grandmother

MARY – What were the stories about?

IRENE – Many things…historical things…wondrous things

ELLEN – Fan fiction before fan fiction was a thing. Can we go now?

IRENE – No! I've waited a long time and come a long way for this.

ELLEN – We're definitely not in New Jersey anymore

MARY – I want to hear one of the stories

ELLEN – Now?

IRENE – I can't think of a better time or place to tell one.

ELLEN – I wish there was some place to sit down

IRENE – And this is one of my favorites

ELLEN – It's too cold!

IRENE – Chances are, you have heard many stories of the exploits of the famous Sherlock Holmes. But there is one story you do not know…one case his associate John Watson did not turn into a sensational tabloid tale. Because some tales are too personal for that. It began at what Holmes *thought* was the end of his career in 1899. Watson, as was his wont had found another preacher that caught his fancy. This one was an American. He led his small flock from a chapel in Camden town…

The Glory to God Church, a humble, storefront place of worship in Camden Town, London – As Watson takes a seat in one of the pews his fellow congregants, a motley lot from the dregs of London society turn and stare before standing and surrounding him.

1899

BERT – *(To Watson)* Yer not from around these parts are ye?

DRUSILA – E's a real snappy dresser e is!

FLORA – Maybe e's lost

NIGEL – *(Fingering Watson's lapel)* Ow much did ye pay for that suit?

FLORA – Keep yer ands to yerself Nigel! Wot's yer name mister?

WATSON – *(Hesitantly)* John Watson

DRUSILLA – Pleased to meet ye' Mr. Watson

WATSON – Doctor

DRUSILLA – Wots that?

WATSON – It's Doctor Watson…not mister.

NIGEL – Well…wot do ye know about that? We've got a doctor among us!

FLORA – *(Putting her hand on Watson's shoulder)* And an 'andsome doctor at that

DRUSILLA – *(Knocking Flora's hand away and replacing it with her own)* Siddown Flora! I seen 'im first

BERT – Both o' ye stop! Wot would the reverend think if e seen ow you two was behaving.'

FLORA – Ere's the reverend now

The congregation sits as Thomas Boston Corbett in the guise of Reverend Richard Thatcher steps to the pulpit and begins preaching

CORBETT – Let us speak now of angels… magnificent, spiritual creatures whose power is so great that just one can destroy an army…whose presence is so awesome that those who see them fall unconscious to the ground. And yet, they can appear to us as human…and… like us… they have free will. So, they can choose good or evil. They can speak the language of heaven or the language of earth. They can be messengers and protectors or tempters and destroyers. Their bright songs can be true or false…they can lead us to eternal salvation or fiery damnation. So…. beware…

A gunshot is heard. Screams are heard from the congregation as Corbett falls to the ground

MADELINE – *(Running to him)* Reverend Thatcher!

WATSON – *(Jumping to his feet and addressing the congregation)* Do not panic! Keep your seats and keep your heads down! *(Leans over Corbett)* Are you hit sir? *(Corbett does not respond and Watson searches for a pulse.)*

DRUSILLA – 'E's dead…They've killed 'im!

NIGEL – 'E always said they would!

WATSON – *(Continuing to examine Corbett)* No…. He's quite alive…and no sign of a wound. I think he's fainted… *(To Corbett)* Reverend? Reverend, can you hear me? Reverend?

CORBETT – *(Suddenly sitting upright and glaring at Watson)* You! …You show your face at last!

WATSON – *(Backing up quickly)* …. What?

CORBETT – Are you in charge?

MADELINE – Try to calm yourself Reverend…. I do not think…

WATSON – No…I'm the physician who came to your aid!

DRUSILLA – *(To Corbett)* It's true

BERT – 'E did!

CORBETT – *(Standing up with a crazed look, he pulls a small pistol from his coat and waves it in the air)* They're still hiding then…afraid to come out of the shadows. I cannot see them…but I can hear them…whispering…murmuring…Why don't they show themselves? WHY DON'T YOU SHOW YOURSELVES?

WATSON – Who are you addressing sir?

CORBETT – Them...the ones who follow me

MADELINE – *(Gently taking the gun from Corbett)* We cannot be sure of that

CORBETT – They never rest...they cannot be escaped!

MADELINE – *(Stepping between Corbett and Watson)* Reverend.... please...I think you have said enough.

The courtyard outside 221 B Baker Street. It is the following morning. Holmes holds a folded copy of the London Times as he and Watson Walk toward the residence

HOLMES – From the way you describe him, this American preacher sounds quite mad Watson.

WATSON – He went on to tell me that these...avengers, as he calls them have been following him since 1865.

HOLMES – They're a persistent lot... *(Unfolding the newspaper)* but this small item in the Times makes no mention of that.

WATSON – Once the gentlemen from the Metropolitan police and the press arrived, Thatcher went quiet. He claimed to have no idea why someone would take a shot at him or who that someone might be. His fellow American acolyte...the young lady I was telling you about... told the same story

HOLMES – And when the police questioned *you*?

WATSON – *(After a pause)* I told them nothing

HOLMES – Why?

WATSON – In my clinical opinion the ravings of a lunatic to a physician should be of no of concern to the police…or the press

HOLMES – Do you believe this man is a lunatic?

WATSON – I'm not sure what I believe. He's either a lunatic or a prophet

HOLMES – In any event you are not his physician

WATSON – In the moment that I came to his aid I *was*. And society's treatment of its insane…and its prophets increases their suffering beyond measure. I will not contribute to that.

HOLMES – Very noble

WATSON – And to be honest I found his sermon quite compelling

HOLMES – Watson, I will never understand your fascination with purveyors of spiritual quackery

WATSON – Not everything unexplainable by your infernal logic is quackery

HOLMES – True…pure fantasy, mindless drivel and the ravings of lunatics are also unexplainable by logic.

WATSON – I had hoped that in retirement you would take time to broaden your horizons

HOLMES – If by taking time to broaden my horizons you mean accompanying you on your pilgrimages to mediums, soothsayers and self-proclaimed prophets...no thank you.

WATSON – Let us just say I have...a mind more open to metaphysical possibilities than you do.

HOLMES – Minds, like front doors, are often improved by a secure lock Watson.

They enter the flat

WATSON – And what about *your* mind? Is *it* improved by morphine?

HOLMES – We're not talking about *my* mind!

WATSON – All minds seek comfort from some source. You've chosen yours to escape the dull routine of existence, now kindly allow me to choose mine to escape something far worse.

HOLMES – *(Sighing)* Watson, I understand...

WATSON – *(Cutting him off)* You do *not* understand! *(Softly)* But, how could you?

HOLMES – *(After a pause)* I am sorry.... I know I have not experienced what you have.... nor seen what you have seen.

So….no…I do not understand your spiritual quest. But I respect it.

WATSON – *(Softly)* Thank you…Holmes *(The doorbell rings but Holmes and Watson pay it no mind)*

The doorbell rings again

HOLMES – Mrs. Hudson! The door! *(The doorbell rings again)* Where in the bloody hell is she? MRS. HUDSON!

MRS. HUDSON – *(Entering from another room, rubbing her eyes)* Were you calling me Mr. Holmes?

The doorbell rings again

HOLMES – Yes, Mrs. Hudson I was calling you… *(The doorbell rings again)* … But the doorbell has been calling you longer

MRS. HUDSON – The doorbell? *(The doorbell rings again)* Oh yes…there it is. What of it?

The doorbell rings again

HOLMES – It's ringing

The doorbell rings again

MRS. HUDSON – So it is

HOLMES – Would you like to answer it?

MRS. HUDSON – Would I like to…? *(Smiling coyly)* Oh! Oh my!

WATSON – *(Gently)* I'll answer it Mrs. Hudson

MRS. HUDSON – Thank you Doctor…such a gentleman.

Watson shoots Holmes a dark look as he exits toward the front door. He opens it to find an attractive, smartly dressed middle aged woman.

WATSON – Good day Madame

ANNA – Is this the residence of Mr. Sherlock Holmes, the consulting detective?

WATSON – It is but…

ANNA – And are you, by any chance, Dr. John Watson?

WATSON – I am.

ANNA – It is an honor to meet you sir. I have read everything you've ever written!

WATSON – Thank you…Madame. I am flattered

ANNA – *(Peering over Watson's shoulder)* Is Mr. Holmes in?

WATSON – Well…Mr. Holmes is not…

ANNA – I am in urgent need of his services sir.

WATSON – I do not think….

ANNA – Please sir…. May I come in?

WATSON Of course…

WATSON – Holmes…. a lady to see you

HOLMES – So I heard. *(To Anna)* Good day Madame. I am Sherlock Holmes. Whom do I have the pleasure of addressing?

ANNA – *(Offering her hand, which Holmes takes in his)* I am Mrs. Anna Tonry Mr. Holmes. I've come from the United States…. *(Unimpressed, Holmes releases her hand)* …from Baltimore…I arrived on the Oceanic two weeks ago.

HOLMES – Why have you come to *me*?

ANNA – Surely you know that your reputation is as well-known on my side of the Atlantic as it is on this one.

HOLMES – Yes…thanks to the incessant scribblings of my associate here, my reputation is known farther and wider than I wish it was

ANNA – Be that as it may, there are criminals at large who must be brought to justice and I have reason to believe that you are the only man who can do it

HOLMES – I am flattered Madam, however….

ANNA – They are part of a conspiracy that must be revealed to the world before it is too late.

HOLMES – I'm afraid it *is* too late

ANNA – What?

HOLMES – Too late for *me* at least

ANNA – What are you saying?

HOLMES – I am retired Madame

ANNA – No…

HOLMES – I am truly sorry you travelled all this way…for no purpose

ANNA – *(Softly, repeating to herself)* No, no no...

HOLMES – I blame Watson for this. His sensational tabloid tales mislead people into thinking I am still taking cases

WATSON – Need I remind you that those sensational tabloid tales pay the rent?

HOLMES – Only until I remove myself to the countryside and my bees

WATSON – You and your…

ANNA – *(In full voice)* NO! *(Holmes and Watson, taken aback look at her in silent surprise for a moment)* You do not understand! Without your help Mr. Holmes a great wrong will go unpunished and men who did unspeakable evil in the shadows will remain in those shadows.

HOLMES – *(To Watson)* You may add to the list of things unexplainable by logic, emotional outbursts by women

ANNA – Despite what you may think Mr. Holmes I am not just some hysterical female. *(To Watson)* And I am not a deluded reader of your stories. I know fact from fiction…and I know that if you do not help me the guilty will go unpunished and the innocent will die unredeemed

HOLMES – Even if that is true Mrs. Tonry, it could have been said of nearly every case in my career…a career that is now ended

ANNA – *(She thinks for moment)* It is sad to think that the world's greatest detective ended his career before he solved the one case that would have *made* that career

WATSON – Mrs. Tonry, under normal circumstances appealing to my friend's vanity would be a sure way to get him to do what you want but I fear he may be beyond that appeal now.

ANNA – It is sadder still to think that a career as great as yours Mr. Holmes will only be recorded in the pulp pages of penny dreadfuls instead of in the immortal pages of history books

WATSON – I do *not* write penny dreadfuls!

HOLMES – *(After a pause)* Are you offering me…*immortality* if I take your case?

18

ANNA –Years ago my mother's honor and life were taken. I am offering you the opportunity to right that wrong.
(Holmes walks away from her, apparently lost in thought)
And I am prepared to pay you handsomely

WATSON – *(Breaking the awkward silence)* Mrs. Tonry, allow me to reiterate, on behalf of my friend that Mr. Holmes is happily retired from taking on new cases and…while we are both sorry for the inconvenience of your long journey…we are…

HOLMES – *(Cutting him off)* …Very interested in hearing more

WATSON – What?

HOLMES – The poor woman has crossed an ocean Watson, the *least* we can do is hear her out.

ANNA – Thank you Mr. Holmes!

HOLMES – Do not thank me. I haven't agreed to anything yet. Surely there are detectives and law enforcement officers in your own country who could help

ANNA – None have ever…. nor ever *will*…be of any help to me. They are part of it!

WATSON – Part of what?

ANNA – A conspiracy that began thirty four years ago.

WATSON – Why the urgency now?

ANNA – *(After a pause)* There are two reasons. For one, my time is short. My doctors tell me that my kidneys are failing and there is nothing they can do for me.

WATSON – I am…very sorry to hear that

HOLMES – Perhaps, if Mrs. Tonry is agreeable, you could examine her and offer an opinion Watson.

WATSON – Of course…If you are agreeable Mrs. Tonry

ANNA – My husband is also a physician, but your learned opinion will be most welcome as well sir. Although I suspect Mr. Holmes is concerned with more than my welfare

HOLMES – What is your other reason?

ANNA – *(Takes a folded newspaper clipping from the small bag she is carrying and hands it to Holmes)* When I saw this in the Times this morning, I knew I had to see you immediately

Holmes reads the clipping for a moment and hands it to Watson

WATSON – *(After glancing at the clipping)* This is the article about the attempted shooting of Revered Thatcher

ANNA– You already know about it?

WATSON – I was…

HOLMES – *(Cutting him off)* For now, let us just say that we are… *aware* of the incident

ANNA – Find who shot at this Reverend Mr. Holmes and you will find the key to the conspiracy.

HOLMES – What does this half mad preacher have to do with your conspiracy?

ANNA– For one thing, this half mad preacher as you call him is not who he claims to be. Richard Thatcher is not even his real name. His real name is Thomas Boston Corbett. *(She pauses to gauge their reaction)* Do you know who that is?

WATSON – A Camden Town preacher with an alias apparently

ANNA – He is the man who killed John Wilkes Booth

HOLMES – The assassin of your president Lincoln

ANNA – Yes…Thomas Boston Corbett was the assassin's, assassin

HOLMES – Or… some might say he was Lincoln's avenger…How have *you* come to know so much about this man?

ANNA – Discovering everything…and *everyone*…connected to Lincoln's death…and Booth's murder has been my life's work

HOLMES – Let us say that Reverend Thatcher is, in reality this Corbett. What does the assault on him have to do with your dark conspiracy?

ANNA – To understand that Mr. Holmes, you need to know who *I* am. *(She pauses)* My maiden name is Surratt.

WATSON – *(After a pause)* Should that mean something to us?

HOLMES – The name Surratt is…intimately connected to the Lincoln assassination… *(To Anna)* ... John Surratt

ANNA – *(Finishing his sentence)* Is my brother, yes

HOLMES – *(To Watson)* John Surratt was a spy for the American Confederacy Watson. He was tried as a co-conspirator

ANNA – And acquitted of all charges

HOLMES – Acquitted does not mean innocent

ANNA – He was not even in Washington on the night of the assassination!

HOLMES – Your mother…on the other hand…

ANNA – *(To Watson)* My mother…. Mary… was convicted and hanged in July 1865

HOLMES – The first…and to date…*only* woman executed by your government

ANNA – An *innocent* woman Mr. Holmes.

HOLMES – Was she?

ANNA – *(Angrily)* She was!

HOLMES – As I recall it, prosecutors claimed that your mother aided and abetted the assassination by carrying messages, hiding weapons and providing a safe house for the conspirators

ANNA – My mother ran a boarding house…

HOLMES – Some even claimed she was the master mind behind the conspiracy

ANNA – Nonsense! Nonsense and lies! The evidence against her was circumstantial. The real conspiracy was the one that sent an innocent woman and anyone else they could round up to the gallows

HOLMES – Why?

ANNA – To ensure their silence

HOLMES – I assume you have some proof of your claim

ANNA – *(Taking a small stack of notebook size pages tied together with a ribbon from her bag)* I do…right here on these pages. What is written on them will not only exonerate my mother, it will change American history.

WATSON – They appear to be pages from a date book.

ANNA – They are diary entries

WATSON – Whose?

ANNA – John Wilkes Booth's

HOLMES – If those pages are what you claim them to be…
why are they significant?

ANNA – Because they reveal a truth that men in high places
want hidden

WATSON – How did *you* come to possess them?

ANNA – I will tell you…in good time…if Mr. Holmes
agrees to take the case

HOLMES – You will tell us now…or I guarantee that I will
not take your case

ANNA – Very well… After Mr. Booth was killed, his diary
was taken to Washington and given to Edwin Stanton, the
Secretary of War who…. if he is to be believed…put it in a
desk drawer and forgot about it.

WATSON – If he is to be believed?

HOLMES – Secretary Stanton was not a man to let truth
interfere with his aims. Go on Madame

ANNA – The diary was not produced as evidence at my
mother's trial in 1865 but it *was* produced at my brother's
trial two years later. By then it had been re-discovered in a
forgotten War Department file…but with pages missing. The

government prevented the diary from being introduced during my mother's trial because it contained things they did not want known. By the time of my brother's trial the pages containing those things were gone.

HOLMES – And you believe those are the missing pages.

ANNA – Yes

WATSON – Who gave them to you?

ANNA – One day when my husband was at his office seeing patients a man called at our home. He would not give his name. He just handed the pages to me and said, "Booth's killer, Corbett lives in London as Richard Thatcher. A consulting detective named Sherlock Holmes lives there as well and he will help you."

HOLMES – You have no idea who this man was?

ANNA – None. All I know is that the truth these pages contain would have saved my mother's life had it been known in 1865

HOLMES – Did you go to the authorities?

ANNA – *(Contemptuously)* Authorities…The day my mother was sentenced to death I tried to see Andrew Johnson, the new president. When I tried to enter the White House two Senators barred the door… Picture it, Mr. Holmes…a sobbing, hysterical girl begging to see the one man who could save her mother's life being coldly restrained. Everyone associated in any way with this crime has been damaged beyond measure. The shadow cast by a dishonored and murdered mother has darkened my entire life. *You* can understand that…can't you Mr. Holmes?

HOLMES – *(Taken aback he pauses a moment before answering)* I will… carefully consider all you have told us in deciding whether to take your case

ANNA – *(She takes a card from her purse and hands it to Holmes)* You may reach me at my hotel. I can see myself out.

She exits

WATSON – A mysterious stranger…missing diary pages…a vast conspiracy… it sounds preposterous

HOLMES – That does not make it untrue

WATSON – And her claims about Reverend Thatcher…still, her arrival a day after the assault on him is an odd coincidence

HOLMES – The probability of it being a coincidence is very slight I'm afraid

WATSON – I thought you were planning to retire

HOLMES – I *am* planning to retire…someday

WATSON – After you are immortalized in history books?

HOLMES – Despite what you think I will not take this case out of vanity

WATSONS – Why then?

HOLMES – I have my reasons

WATSON – What are they?

HOLMES – Curiosity for one…and another…more personal reason that I would rather not discuss at present

WATSON – Very well…Why didn't you ask her what was written on those diary pages?

HOLMES – What is written on those pages is of no consequence until I have established Mrs. Tonry's credibility

WATSON – How will you do that?

HOLMES – Not I Watson…*we.* First, I want *you* to pay a call on your friend the Reverend and endeavor to learn who he really is

WATSON – Why me?

HOLMES – He knows you. He's more likely to trust you. After you have spoken with the Reverend call on Mrs. Tonry at her hotel and conduct the physical examination to which she agreed. *(He begins to exit)* I will see you in three days Watson

WATSON – Where are you going?

HOLMES – Out

WATSON – What are you going to do?

HOLMES – I am going to take up the study of London current events and American history.

The Glory to God Church. Watson enters from the shadows in the back of the church

NIGEL – Well…look who's back.

DRUSILLA – It's the brave doctor.

FLORA – Brave and 'andsome

MADELINE – *(Entering)* Who is it? Who is there?

WATSON – John Watson.

MADELINE – *(Cautiously)* Dr. Watson… It is…good to see you sir.

WATSON – I don't believe we've ever been formally introduced

MADELINE – *(Offering Watson her hand)* My name is Madeline Hughes

WATSON – *(Taking her hand)* I am pleased to officially make your acquaintance Miss Hughes.

MADELINE – It's Mrs. actually

WATSON – Mrs. Hughes…I have come to call on Reverend Thatcher. Is he here?

MADELINE – I expect him at any moment. *(To Flora)* Will you please leave.

NIGEL – That's not very Christian if you ask me

MADELINE – No one asked you

FLORA – It's cold outside.

DRUSILLA – We was just tryin' to keep warm

MADELINE – *(Pushing her to the door)* You can keep warm somewhere else. The service begins at seven. You can come back then.

She walks back to Watson

WATSON – How long have you known the Reverend?

MADELINE – I have…been…with him for two years

WATSON – It would appear that you are more than just a member of his flock

MADELINE – I do what I can to aid him in his work…and look after him. If it is not too impertinent of me to ask, what is your business with him?

WATSON – *(Hesitantly)* My business?

MADELINE – If it is not too impertinent of me to ask

WATSON – No…no of course not I…I…ummm

MADELINE – The Reverend is a very busy man

WATSON – I'm sure he is

MADELINE – And a very private man. He socializes with very few people.

WATSON – I see *(Corbett enters from the back of the church. Watson moves toward him, extending his hand)* Reverend Thatcher! It is good to see you looking so well sir

CORBETT – You are…the doctor? …

WATSON – Dr. John Watson…yes

CORBETT – *(Taking Watson's hand)* Being told I appear well by a medical man is surely a good thing.

WATSON – I was wondering if I might take a few moments of you time.

MADELINE – I explained to Dr. Watson that you are very busy and that you do not…

CORBETT – It is alright Madeline.

MADELINE – But…

CORBETT – *(Placing a hand on her arm)* Leave us now…we have nothing to fear from this man.

Madeline reluctantly exits

WATSON – *(After an awkward moment)* I must say…you appear very different from the way you did the last time I saw you.

CORBETT – That's because I *was* different. I was carried away by the spirit then

WATSON – Carried away by the spirit?

CORBETT – It is difficult to explain in words…the spirit…comes upon me all at once. It is overwhelming, and it makes me very certain about what seems uncertain to most men. When the spirit comes upon me and I am in the presence of goodness, I have no doubt and know no fear. I only feel those things in the presence of evil. Is that what you have come to see me about?

WATSON – No… *(Watson turns away for a moment then turns back and speaks)* …Reverend, when a man experiences something that destroys his faith…in God…and in himself…can he ever regain it?

CORBETT – That would depend on the man… and what he experienced. Have a seat, Doctor. *(He guides Watson into a pew and sits beside him)*

WATSON – *(Hesitantly at first)* During the Afghan War I was an assistant surgeon with the Berkshires Sixty Sixth Foot. Once we were sent to break up an enemy patrol coming through the Maiwand Pass…But it wasn't a patrol… It was the main force. *(He stops…seemingly unable to continue)*

CORBETT – *(Gently)* What happened?

WATSON – It was a slaughter. I was wounded…hit in the shoulder… The Afghans kept firing at us … until only eleven were left standing…. And those…brave men… did not retreat…did not surrender. They charged…I can still see them being swallowed up in the smoke…and when the smoke cleared… *(practically weeping)* I should have been among them.

CORBETT – You feel shame for surviving?

WATSON – I feel shame for not acting honorably

CORBETT – You were wounded

WATSON – In the shoulder! I could still walk!

CORBETT – And you think honor demanded that you sacrifice your life?

WATSON – The eleven did!

CORBETT – They did their duty as they saw it…

WATSON – And a just, merciful God allowed it?

CORBETT – He allowed each man to make his own choice.

WATSON – Before that day I was certain I would have made the same choice

CORBETT – *(Thinks for a moment and places his hand gently on Watson's shoulder)* You and I Doctor…we're both old soldiers you know.

WATSON – You were a military man?

CORBETT – If my father hadn't taken me to America when I was a boy, I would have fought for the Crown myself.

WATSON – You're a native Englishman? *(Corbett nods)*

CORBETT – The war against Southern secession…that was the war *I* signed on for.

WATSON – Were you a minister before you enlisted?

CORBETT – I was a hat maker…and a drunk.

WATSON – Oh…

CORBETT – After my wife died, I crawled into a whiskey bottle…didn't come out until the night some Christians found me in a Boston gutter. Thanks to them I was saved and from then on, I knew whether I was a…. hat maker or a soldier or a preacher…my *mission* was to save souls…I enlisted when the war started.

WATSON – Did you see action?

CORBETT – Some. Antietam……Gettysburg.

WATSON – Your enemy made a glorious charge at Gettysburg…and you a glorious repulse

CORBETT – I saw very little glory in my war Doctor

WATSON – I wish I could say the same.

CORBETT – Once…a group of us were out foraging and we were ambushed by Confederate cavalry. We ran for the woods. Most of the men gave up right away. But I found a good spot in a shallow ditch and whenever a Rebel came near me, I'd fire...held them off for hours. Until finally, one man, made it through and knocked the rifle out of my hand. He was about to shoot me on the spot when his commander shouted, "Don't shoot that man. He has a right to defend himself." *(Pausing...with a smile)* Sometimes my guardian Angels come to me in unexpected forms. After that they put me with the others and sent us to Andersonville.

WATSON – You are a courageous man. When you were tested you acted honorably

CORBETT – My war is fought, Doctor. But I fear another is in your future. *(Watson abruptly turns away from him)*

WATSON – *(Changing the subject)* Reverend...there is another question I must ask you. Is Richard Thatcher your real name?

CORBETT – Is that important?

WATSON – I know a man who can help you...but he must know your true identity. Is your name Thomas Corbett?

CORBETT – My name is *Boston* Corbett. I took the name of the city where my soul was saved!

WATSON – Why do you call yourself Richard Thatcher?

CORBETT – To hide from...them.

WATSON – I must ask one more question. Is it true that you are the man who shot John Wilkes Booth?

CORBETT – *(Looks wide eyed at Watson for a long moment)* It is

WATSON – Will you tell me about it?

CORBETT – I had hoped never to tell of it again.

WATSON – I am sorry but…

CORBETT – *(Cutting him off)* There are some crosses we can never put down! …I re-enlisted after my release from Andersonville

WATSON – Good God! Why?

CORBETT – The war wasn't over. Ten days after Lincoln was killed, I was picked to join a detachment going to Virginia to search for Booth. We found him… hiding in a tobacco barn. I was near a crack in one of the walls…I had my pistol aimed at Booth when… I heard a voice…a loud, clear voice…and it said, "God's will be done." I was turning around to see who had spoken when I saw Booth raise *his* pistol. The voice spoke again…a whisper this time "God's will be done." I fired. When the assassin lay dead, I knew God had used me to avenge Abraham Lincoln.

WATSON – These people who will not show themselves. Do you believe they are trying to avenge *Booth's* death?

CORBETT – Every death its own avenger breeds. Can the man you know really help me, Doctor?

WATSON – I believe he can. I will be in touch shortly. Until then, be safe Reverend. Good day sir

Watson exits. Corbett paces, still in an agitated state. After a few moments ethereal murmuring is heard.

CORBETT – Who is it? Who's there? (*The murmuring gets louder. He covers his ears*) WHY WON'T YOU SHOW YOURSELVES?!

A woman's voice, low and husky emerges from the murmuring

VOICE – Thomas?

CORBETT – Yes?

VOICE – Thomas?

CORBETT – I hear you…I hear you

VOICE – Thomas…don't you know me?

CORBETT – No…who are you?

VOICE – It is me Thomas…Susan

CORBETT – Susan….

VOICE – Susan Rebecca…Your wife. Do you not know my voice?

CORBETT – It has been many years…

VOICE – I have been watching over you

CORBETT – Watching over me….

VOICE – Protecting you

CORBETT – Where are you?

VOICE – Heaven of course

CORBETT – Heaven

VOICE – I have missed you. But very soon we will be together. The time has come for you to join me…for eternity

CORBETT – *(With tears in his eyes)* For eternity

VOICE – Will you come to me?

CORBETT – Yes

Corbett removes his pistol from inside his coat and raises it to his temple. Madeline enters and rushes to him

MADELINE – Reverend! NO! *(She grabs the pistol from his hand)*

CORBETT – Susan! Susan? Please answer me! Susan, I am sorry!

He collapses into Madeline's arms

A London library. Holmes and Watson walk among the stacks

WATSON – And that is how the Reverend came to be in England

HOLMES – Good work Watson. Now, on to the matter of Mrs. Tonry's health.

WATSON – She was telling the truth. She is not a well woman

HOLMES – Is her condition terminal?

WATSON – It is

HOLMES – How long does she have?

WATSON – With proper care, six to twelve months at most. You *still* haven't told me what *you* have been doing for the past three days

HOLMES – I've been in disguise

WATSON – As what?

HOLMES – A murderer for hire. If a band of conspirators had targeted the Reverend to be killed it should be known within the circles of the London underworld

WATSON – And *is* it known?

HOLMES – No. If Mrs. Tonry's conspiracy exists it is well concealed. When I was *not* consorting with criminals, I was here…rounding out my knowledge of Lincoln assassination conspiracy theories

WATSON – How many are there?

HOLMES – Several…some quite fanciful…others more plausible

WATSON – I thought the facts of the assassination were straightforward. Booth, a well-known American actor and Confederate sympathizer shot the president during a performance in a Washington theater.

HOLMES – Watson, you have been with me long enough to know that crimes themselves are only observable acts. To understand and solve them one must discover their causes and motivations.

WATSON – Yes…quite true

HOLMES – It is difficult for people to accept that a controversial political leader like Lincoln could be eliminated at the whim an actor and a handful of Confederate malcontents

WATSON – Controversial? I thought Mr. Lincoln was a beloved figure to the Americans

HOLMES – He is now…to some. But in his time, he was a most hated man

WATSON – By the Confederates…of course.

HOLMES – And by many of his northern countrymen as well

WATSON – Why?

HOLMES – Mr. Lincoln was an ambitious…some have even said…ruthless politician. He adopted a noble cause but in the name of that cause he violently silenced his opponents, jailed his enemies without charge, seized property without compensation and denied his disaffected countrymen the right to self-determination they had rebelled against the Crown to secure. He may be a revered figure in America today but in 1865 he had more enemies than friends. People demand a complex explanation for the murder of such a man…hence the conspiracy theories

WATSON – Do you believe any of them?

HOLMES – I do not know what to believe. Besides, there is one we have not heard yet.

They exit the library

The street outside the library

A wild eyed woman, wearing a sash that says "Repent" is making her rounds.

REPENT WOMAN – *(Shouting to the world)* Repent! Repent! The end is near! Repent now while there is still time!

As Holmes and Watson pass her, she stops abruptly and steps into Holmes' path

REPENT WOMAN – *(Staring wide eyed at Holmes)* – You! It's you!

HOLMES – Madame, if have no business with you.

REPENT WOMAN – *(To Holmes)* Only you can save them!

HOLMES – *(Pushing past her)* – Please let us pass.

REPENT WOMAN – *(Calling after him)* – Only you can save them!

WATSON – What do you suppose that was all about?

HOLMES – Nothing

WATSON – Nothing?

HOLMES – Watson, sometimes a lunatic is just a lunatic.

The residence, 221B Baker Street

HOLMES – By the way Watson, during my hiatus I paid a call on our old friend Inspector Lestrade

WATSON – Whatever for? You're not involving *him* in this matter, are you?

HOLMES – No…But he was able to loan me this photograph of Booth's handwriting. *(He removes the photograph from his jacket pocket and hands it to Watson)*

WATSON – *(Looking at the photograph)* Where did he get this?

HOLMES – Scotland Yard received it from the American Secret Service. *(He takes the photograph back from Watson)* Governments see great value in reciprocity when it comes to sharing information about assassins. *(The doorbell rings)* Ahhh, that must be Mrs. Tonry. I sent for her.

Mrs. Hudson enters

MRS. HUSDON – Mr. Holmes?

HOLMES – Yes, Mrs. Hudson

MRS. HUDSON – *(In a stage whisper)* There's a lady here to see you!

WATSON – Why are you whispering?

MRS. HUDSON – I do not wish to be indiscreet…

HOLMES – Is this lady the same one who was here several days ago?

MRS. HUDSON – Well I…I do not know sir

HOLMES – Had you answered the doorbell you would.

MRS. HUDSON – Yes…I suppose so. But may I remind you…once again…I am not your maid!

HOLMES – Yes, yes, yes…you have made that abundantly clear. *(There is an awkward moment)* Well….show her in.

MRS. HUDSON – *(Sarcastically)* Oh yes sir…right away sire…Tea sir? *(As Holmes and Watson shake their heads she goes to the door, emerging a moment later with Anna)* Right through there Ma'am

ANNA – Thank you

WATSON – *(Nodding in greeting)* Mrs. Tonry

ANNA – Doctor Watson *(walking to Holmes)* Mr. Holmes. I have brought the diary pages as you requested. *(Taking the pages from her bag and handing them to Holmes)* Have you decided to take my case?

HOLMES – You will know by the time our interview is concluded *(He closely examines the photograph of Booth's handwriting and the diary pages)* I have compared the handwriting on these pages with a sample of John Wilkes Booths' handwriting

ANNA – And?

HOLMES – The comparison told me what I needed to know. Now, will you summarize the facts of the conspiracy that are described on these pages?

ANNA – Very well…The first thing you need to know is that John Wilkes Booth was not a murderer. He was a Southern patriot. When his country was invaded, he acted in her defense.

HOLMES – By the time he acted his country no longer existed

ANNA – In his heart it did….and he had a good heart.

WATSON – You knew him?

ANNA – *(Looking away)* We met…yes…at my mother's boardinghouse.

HOLMES – You were fond of him?

ANNA – History has judged him for what he *did*. I remember him for the *man* he was…a gentle man…a man of honor. The same cannot be said of the conspirators who instigated his act

HOLMES – And who were they?

ANNA – Investors in New York and London, the Confederate Secretary of State…high officials in the Union War Department…members of *your* Parliament.

WATSON – Members of Parliament?

ANNA – And the Crown was aware of it!

WATSON – Absurd!

ANNA – Not absurd Doctor…logical! Cotton meant money and money meant power. The South grew the cotton your country needed. You had the power the South needed, and northern investors had the money to pay for it.

HOLMES – How did this logical strategy work…specifically?

ANNA – Cotton investors in New York sent money through a network of Confederate spies to cotton investors in England. They used the money to bribe Members of Parliament to support diplomatic recognition of the Confederacy. But it didn't work. When the South was on the verge of defeat and the investors were on the verge of bankruptcy the conspirators conceived a final mission, and they chose John Wilkes Booth to perform it.

HOLMES – Why Booth?

ANNA – His fame gave him a free pass to travel anywhere without arousing suspicion

HOLMES – And what was this final mission?

ANNA – The kidnapping of Lincoln

WATSON – Kidnapping a president?

ANNA – So he could be ransomed.

WATSON – For money?

ANNA – For Union recognition of the Confederacy

WATSON – What an audacious scheme.

ANNA – It would have ended the war and saved the cotton market in one stroke. Mr. Booth recruited my brother and the others to help him…with a *kidnapping*…not an assassination! My brother offered him the use of my mother's boarding house as a place for them to meet…nothing more.

HOLMES – Your mother consented to this of course.

ANNA – Yes but…

HOLMES – And she was aware of what was being planned

ANNA – To be honest Mr. Holmes I do not know what my mother knew…but I know she was not a murderer

HOLMES – *(After a pause)* What did *you* know?

ANNA – Nothing!

HOLMES – You said that you and Mr. Booth were acquainted. Surely you spoke

ANNA – Not about his plans. The kidnapping attempts failed…one after another. Then Lee surrendered, and the mission changed… from abduction to assassination

HOLMES – Why? The war was lost, and Mr. Lincoln was willing to offer generous terms

ANNA – That I do not know. And neither did Mr. Booth. He was a soldier, not a general. But it was his opinion that Lincoln's own War Department betrayed him.

HOLMES – That's quite an assertion How was this betrayal carried out?

ANNA – *(She takes the diary pages from Holmes and reads from them)* "There were no soldiers patrolling the front of the theater, no police backstage and no sentries guarding the presidential box. The old tyrant was posed before me like a target."

WATSON – How is Corbett involved?

ANNA – Don't you find it odd that the army could not capture a trapped cripple alive? Dead men tell no tales Mr. Holmes. Thomas Boston Corbett was the gunman the conspirators chose to eliminate Booth and they have been trying to eliminate *him* ever since

HOLMES – More than thirty years have passed. Most of the conspirators must be dead by now

ANNA – Most but not all. Discover who is trying to harm Corbett and you will discover who is still hiding the truth that killed my mother. Now…once and for all Mr. Holmes… will you take this case?

HOLMES – *(After pacing for a long moment)* No

ANNA – *(Incredulous)* Why not?!

HOLMES – For one thing these diary pages are forged

ANNA – No…

HOLMES – I'm not saying *you* forged them. *(He holds up the photograph of Booth's handwriting)* In fact, I am quite certain the forger was a man. He was quite skillful too…but not skillful enough to fool me. The other reason I will not take your case is the fraudulent story you told

ANNA – Are you calling me a fraud?

HOLMES – No…*you* may be quite sincere but whoever wrote these pages concocted them from volumes of historical speculation readily available in any decently stocked library…where, no doubt he also found a copy of the genuine passages from Booth's diary that he combined with the one's he invented.

ANNA – That would be very damning Mr. Holmes…if I believed you.

HOLMES – You doubt me?

ANNA – Doctor Watson's stories tell of your expertise in handwriting analysis, but they are mere stories. You say the conspiracy described in these pages could be found in library books. That doesn't make it untrue. And what of the fact that pages that went missing from Booth's diary? You cannot deny that.

HOLMES – I do *not* deny it... *(Holds up the pages)* But that does make these the missing pages

ANNA – I was wrong about you Mr. Holmes

HOLMES – How so?

ANNA – You are not incorruptible…far from it. Perhaps your previous service to the Crown has rendered you incapable of going where the truth leads

HOLMES – Where truth leads, I follow Madame

ANNA – Then follow this… *(She removes two folded pages from her bag and hands them to Holmes who opens the first one and reads it)*

WATSON – What is it Holmes? You've gone pale *(Holmes hands the page to Watson)* It's a family tree

HOLMES – Where did you get this?

ANNA – I'm afraid I was not entirely forthcoming when I told you my anonymous gentleman caller only gave me the diary pages. He gave me that family tree and what I just handed to you as well. I had hoped I would not have to use them to persuade you

WATSON – What is she saying Holmes?

ANNA – If you look closely at that family tree you will see that John Wilkes Booth's mother's maiden name was Mary Anne… *Holmes.*

HOLMES – It's true. She was my father's older sister, making her my aunt

WATSON – Good God Holmes…. The means John Wilkes Booth was…

HOLMES – My cousin…. Yes Watson. My father's family disowned my aunt after she ran off to America with Booth's father Junius. He was already married with a child at the time.

WATSON – You never told me

ANNA – He never told *anyone* Doctor…and for a good reason. Everyone associated in any way with this crime has been damaged beyond measure. My association through my mother has been bad enough. It's been far worse for Mr. Booth's brothers, and they are only actors. I cannot imagine what it will do to the reputation of the world's most famous consulting detective.

WATSON – This is blackmail! How dare you! Holmes? *(Holmes is preoccupied, reading the second page Anna handed to him)* Say something!

ANNA – I'm afraid your friend is feeling a bit overwhelmed at the moment

WATSON – By what?

ANNA – He has just been reminded of something even more disturbing than the identity of his cousin. *(To Holmes)* In light of these new facts I ask you to reconsider your decision…lest they become public knowledge. In fact, if you want your secrets to remain secrets you must not only take this case you must publicize the fact.

WATSON – What? Why?

ANNA – The fact that Sherlock Holmes himself has agreed to take on the conspiracy will drive the rats from the bowels of the sinking ship… *(To Holmes)* Your name will scare them into the light.

WATSON – Or scare them deeper into hiding

ANNA – We shall see what we shall see. *(To Holmes)* Meanwhile, *I* shall expect to see your answer published in the Times within twenty-four hours. If I do not, I will publish what I have learned about you. The shadow cast by a dishonored and murdered mother darkens your entire life…doesn't it, Mr. Holmes?

Anna exits

WATSON – What is it? *(Holmes paces and says nothing)* Will you speak to me?!

HOLMES – *(Agitated, still pacing)* When I was a boy my brother Mycroft and I were tutored by a professor. Over time the professor became… *involved* with my mother

WATSON – Involved?

HOLMES – *(Abruptly)* Involved in an adulterous affair! When my father learned of it, he became mentally unstable…so much so that he…he…murdered my mother

WATSON – My God…

HOLMES – He was acquitted of murder by reason of insanity and committed to an asylum where he later died

WATSON – *(Softly)* What a horror it must have been for you

HOLMES – A horror…yes. And I have been horrified of the murderous blood that flows through my veins ever since

WATSON – Murderous blood?

HOLMES – It's in the lineage Watson! My father…All of my aunt's children…my cousins… were unhinged in one way or another…the assassin was just the worst of the lot. They could not escape their heritage, and neither can I!

WATSON – Holmes, I have known you for years. You are the sanest man I have ever met!

HOLMES – Only through sheer force of will!

WATSON – And your will is without peer…as is your logic and your power of reason

HOLMES – I live in a world of logic and reason devoid of emotion, yes. You have pointed that out many times

WATSON – What I was trying to say was…

HOLMES – My world is devoid of emotion because I *fear* emotion. And the emotion I fear the most is anger…I am full of it…It is in the blood! I am afraid that if I let my guard down…even for a moment…that anger will overtake me as it did my father…as it did Booth. I do not resort to the comforts of morphine to escape the dull routine of existence Watson. I use it to relieve the mental exhaustion I feel from holding the madness at bay

WATSON – My friend…I am a doctor; I know something of blood. And I know that your blood has not determined the man you are. Life has tested you severely and often…beginning when you were just a boy…and you have met each test honorably.

HOLMES – But Watson…don't you see…my life…it's been ruled by fear…fear and anger. I developed my powers of reason because I feared lunacy…I fought crime because my father…and my cousin…were criminals.

WATSON – If Sigmund Freud is to be believed, fear and anger are the wellsprings of all human behavior. *(Holmes laughs hysterically)* Perhaps he is right.

HOLMES – Watson…. look at me! *(He breaks down and weeps)*

WATSON – *(Goes to Holmes' lab table, opens a drawer, takes out a syringe and holds it out to Holmes)* Go ahead then. *(Holmes takes the syringe, looks at it for a long moment and slowly puts it back in the drawer)* You see…*you* choose your actions. And you have always chosen to do good.

HOLMES – For the wrong reasons

WATSON – The reasons do not matter. How many cases have you solved with the deductive reasoning you perfected to safeguard your sanity? How many innocent lives have been saved and protected because you dedicated your life to fighting crime? *(Holmes slowly regains control and stares at him)* You have controlled your life…not fear and anger…you!

HOLMES – *(After a pause, calmer)* Thank you for the words of comfort and assurance Watson. Still…when I think of what that control has cost me. *(He walks to his desk, opens a drawer and takes out a framed photograph. After a moment he hands it to Watson)*

WATSON – Irene Adler

HOLMES – The face of the most beautiful of women and the mind of the most resolute of men. The only woman I could call my equal. The only woman I ever…

WATSON – Ever what?

HOLMES – Meeting a woman like that is a chance that only comes once in a lifetime Watson . *(He abruptly takes the photograph from Watson and puts it back in the desk drawer)* In any event, I look forward to whatever you and Dr. Freud can teach me about the inner workings of my mind. At present, however we have other priorities

WATSON – What are you going to do about Mrs. Tonry's threat?

HOLMES – Nothing. If she publishes what she knows, so be it. I am retired, remember? The peace that will come from being shunned by society will be a welcome relief.

WATSON – Yes…and you *are* still retired Holmes. You did *not* take the case

HOLMES – True…but it appears to have taken us. In any event, the only threat I am concerned with now is the threat to your Reverend… a threat from who or what I *still* cannot say

WATSON – Do you believe that Mrs. Tonry's real motive is the restoration of her mother's honor?

HOLMES – I have never believed that. In my experience, women are motivated by love more than honor

WATSON – I do not doubt that she loved her mother but…

HOLMES – Not *that* kind of love

WATSON – Oh…really?

HOLMES – You heard the way she talked about Booth

WATSON – Yes…awfully sympathetic to the man whose crime led to her mother's death

HOLMES – Yes…awfully…even if she believes he was merely the tool of a larger conspiracy

WATSON – Do you believe her story about the anonymous old gentleman

The doorbell rings

HOLMES – That is the *one* thing she has told us that I *do* believe

WATSON – Who do you suppose he is?

Mrs. Hudson enters

MRS. HUDSON – *(Rushing in)* Doctor Watson?

WATSON – What is it Mrs. Hudson?

MRS. HUDSON – There's a young lady here to see you. She seems quite upset!

WATSON – Show her in please

MRS. HUDSON – He's right in there, Miss

Madeline enters

MADELINE – *(Breathless)* Dr. Watson I… *(She sees Holmes)* Oh…I am sorry I did not realize you already had a guest

WATSON – This is not a guest. This is my flat mate and associate Sherlock Holmes

MADELINE – *(Awestruck)* Oh…Oh my… Sherlock Holmes…*the* Sherlock Holmes?

HOLMES – *(Returning her awestruck gaze with an awestruck gaze of his own)* Yes Madame.

MADELINE – *(To Watson)* And you…you're *that* Dr. Watson…I never made the connection

WATSON – Holmes, this is Madeline Hughes…the young lady from the Reverend's congregation I have told you about

HOLMES – *(Extending his hand)* A pleasure to meet you

WATSON – What can we do for you?

MADELINE – It's the Reverend. He needs your help. I know he trusts you, Doctor Watson. That's why I came

HOLMES – What kind of help?

MADELINE – I'm afraid he's going to kill himself

HOLMES – Why?

MADELINE – I don't know. I have stopped him in the act twice. Something appears to have taken over his mind. I was hoping that the Doctor could help him before it's too late. Will you come with me now to see him?

HOLMES – Of course. Let's go Watson

The Glory to God Church

Corbett is pacing...looking wild eyed

CORBETT – Susan? Are you here? I have come at the appointed hour as we agreed. Susan?

DRUSILLA – *(Sitting with the rest of the congregants in a darkened back pew)* What's the Reverend goin' on about?

NIGEL – I think 'es daft

BERT – It takes one to know one

NIGEL – Shut it!

FLORA – Pipe down the two o' ye

A woman, dressed in white, her face covered enters

WOMAN – Thomas...

NIGEL – It's a bleedin' ghost!

DRUSILLA – Quiet!

CORBETT – Susan!

WOMAN – *(Slowly approaching Corbett)* Are you ready?

CORBETT – Yes...

WOMAN – Show me. *(Corbett takes his pistol from his coat pocket and holds it out to her)*

FLORA – *(Alarmed)* Wot's 'e gonna do with that gun?

CORBETT – Have you come to take me to…to

WOMAN – To heaven…yes Thomas *(She takes the pistol from him and cocks it)* Are you ready?

CORBETT – I am afraid

WOMAN – There is nothing to fear

CORBETT – Why am I afraid?

WOMAN – I do not know my love

CORBETT – Heaven is a certainty

WOMAN – Yes *(She raises the pistol to Corbett's head)*

CORBETT – Then why do I doubt?

WOMAN – There is no reason to. I am here. I love you. Come with me now

CORBETT – *(Shouting)*WHY DO I DOUBT? WHY DO I FEEL FEAR?

WATSON – *(Shouting from the back of the church)* BECAUSE YOU ARE IN THE PRESENCE OF EVIL!

WOMAN – *(Pointing the pistol she looks toward the back of the church)* Who is that? Who is there?

Holmes enters, unseen by the woman and comes up behind her

HOLMES – Put down the gun! *(He rips the veil from her head)* Mrs. Tonry!

Watson and Madeline enter from the back of the church

ANNA – *(Swinging the pistol wildly in front of her. At the back of the church the congregants dive under the pew)* Stay back! Stay back! *(She points the pistol at Corbett)* COME A STEP CLOSER AND HE DIES! I mean it! DO NOT TEST ME MR. HOLMES!

HOLMES – I wouldn't dream of it

ANNA – *(Grinning crazily)* I've beaten you, haven't I?

HOLMES – Apparently… You win

ANNA – I always knew I would…one way or the other

HOLMES – If you wouldn't mind telling me…*what* have you won?

ANNA – REVENGE!

HOLMES – Against?

ANNA – *(Jabbing the gun at Corbett)* HIM!

HOLMES – For what?

ANNA – For killing the only man I have ever loved!

HOLMES – Did he love you in return?

ANNA – Yes…

HOLMES – How do you know?

ANNA – We were to be married

HOLMES – When?

ANNA – After he struck for his country and escaped, I was to join him in Mexico. From there we were to sail away just as his father and mother did when they fled England for America. *(turning suddenly on Corbett)* BUT THIS MURDERER KILLED HIM IN COLD BLOOD TO INSURE HIS SILENCE!

She holds the gun against Corbett's head and seems about to pull the trigger

HOLMES – *(Distracting her)* THERE IS ONE MORE THING *(Anna turns to him and lowers the gun)* …one more thing you could clear up for me Mrs. Tonry Were you aware that a photograph of Mr. Booth's fiancé was found in his diary?

ANNA – What?

HOLMES – There were photographs of five women found in it to be precise.

ANNA – What? What do you mean?

HOLMES – I mean, there were pictures of four actresses…no strike that…*three* actresses, one prostitute and his fiancé found in the diary

ANNA – So? The other pictures mean nothing. I know he had a photograph of me

HOLMES – But it wasn't a photograph of you…It was a photograph of his fiancé…Lucy Hale

ANNA – No

HOLMES – *(Taking a photograph from his pocket)* I have a copy of it here if you would like to see it

ANNA – No!

HOLMES – *(Holding up the photograph)* Lucy Hale

ANNA – EVERYTHING SHE EVER SAID ABOUT HIM…ABOUT THEM…WAS A LIE!

HOLMES – Her mourning of his death appeared very sincere

ANNA – ENOUGH OF YOUR TRICKS! Stop trying to distract me *(She puts the pistol to Corbett's head again)*

WATSON – MADAM!

ANNA – *(Swinging the gun toward Watson)* SILENCE!

WATSON – What happens after you have had your...revenge? You can't escape, and you can't kill all of us

ANNA – *(Looking panicked)* After I send him to hell, I will kill myself

WATSON – If this was your intent all along why were you so insistent that Holmes take your case?

HOLMES – It provided her with cover Watson.

WATSON – Cover?

HOLMES – Until now she thought she could have her revenge and get away with it. Mrs. Tonry knew the mysterious suicide...or murder...of someone connected to the Lincoln assassination would cast suspicion on any member of the Surratt family who just *happened* to be in England when it occurred. But if it was publicly known that she was here to hire *me* to investigate a threat to the Reverend, she would appear innocent

WATSON – *(To Anna)* You must have known that Holmes would eventually expose you

HOLMES – By the time I did she hoped to be home in America where she could die in her own bed instead of in prison...or at the end of a rope

ANNA – So I die here instead. That does not matter...as long as I die knowing THE MURDERER DIED BY MY HAND! *She points the gun at Corbett. Suddenly, Watson rushes in front of Corbett as she pulls the trigger and the gun fires. Madeline runs up behind Anna and grabs the gun from her hand. With her other hand she reaches under her coat and takes out a pair of handcuffs which she places on Anna's wrists*

DRUSILLA – *(Cowering with tother congregants behind a pew)* What happened?

FLORA – I can't look

MADELINE – *(In an authoritative, British accented voice completely different from the American accented one she has used up until now)* Are you alright Doctor?

NIGEL – *(Still under the pew)* Blimey…'who's that?

The congregants peek over the top of the pew

FLORA – It's Miss Madeline

DRUSILLA – That didn't *sound* like Miss Madeline

ANNA – *(Struggling)* Let me go! DAMN YOU!

WATSON – *(Shaken)* I…appear to be fine…but how…

CORBETT – Sometimes my Guardian Angels come to me in unexpected forms *(To Watson)* My prayers for you have been answered Doctor

WATSON – *(Still in shock)* Prayers…for me?

CORBETT – When the moment came you fulfilled your mission with honor sir. *(He offers*

*Watson a crisp, military salute and Watson returns it,
slowly.*

ANNA – DAMN YOU!

CORBETT – *(Turning to Holmes)* Thank you for coming to
my aid sir. *(He shakes Holmes' hand and pauses to look at
him closely)* I can see you are tired but please do not put
your cross down yet. *(To the congregants)* All of you there
in the back. I see you. It's time to go now

*Corbett exits, followed by the congregants as Watson looks
on in wonder*

FLORA – *(Flirtatiously over her shoulder as she exits)*
Goodbye Doctor

WATSON – Goodbye…*(After Corbett and the congregants
have left)* Holmes? …. Did you somehow find a way to put
blanks in that gun?

MADELINE – I did it. This is the Reverend's gun and I
never allow him to have real bullets

ANNA – DAMN ALL OF YOU TO HELL!

MADELINE – *(Slapping Anna hard)* QUIET! …We have
heard all we need to hear from you! *(Anna begins sobbing
quietly)* Doctor…Mr. Holmes I'm afraid I owe you both an
explanation and another introduction. I am Madeline
Hughes…special agent for her Majesty

HOLMES – *(Incredulous, impressed and attracted)* A
woman?

MADELINE – Highly irregular…I know. My husband was the agent assigned to the Revered until he was killed in the line of duty two years ago. Because the Reverend already knew and trusted me it was decided that I should take the job…at least for a while

HOLMES – What is your…job?

MADELINE – I do many things for the Reverend…I'm his bodyguard, his protector…his caretaker

HOLMES – And you are employed by The Crown to do these things?

MADELINE – Yes

HOLMES – Why?

MADELINE – The Crown is very indebted to Reverend Corbett for services he rendered many years ago. Out of gratitude Her Majesty committed to protecting his safety for as long as he lives. There were others who did it before my husband and me. The first ones in America, the rest of us here

WATSON – Does the Reverend know this?

MADELINE – Heavens no! He believes we have all been his Guardian Angels…I suspect he thinks you are one now as well Doctor *(To Holmes)* So sorry for not communicating all of this to you sooner Mr. Holmes. I had no idea you were involved with the Reverend until I met you earlier today.

HOLMES – What is Her Majesty indebted to the Reverend for?

MADELINE – I have no idea. That is something known only to Her Majesty and her ministers I suppose

HOLMES – What do you know of Mrs. Tonry?

MADELINE – Far less than you do I imagine. I didn't even know she existed until we arrived here. I only knew that something was very wrong with the Reverend and that his new-found friend the Doctor might be able to help me figure out what it was. I'll turn her over to Scotland Yard and let them sort things out. They will probably want to talk with *you* Mr. Holmes

HOLMES – I have no doubt

MADELINE – Well…thank you both for your help. Good day gentlemen. *(To Anna as she pulls her hard by the arm)* Come on you!

Madeline and Anna exit

HOLMES – *(Looking to where Madeline and Anna have exited)* Mrs. Hughes bears a striking resemblance to…

WATSON – I know

HOLMES – It's uncanny

WATSON – Never mind about that…what just happened?

HOLMES – *(Still looking to where the women exited)* I admit I am still trying to figure that out myself

They exit the church

A garden courtyard near the Glory to God Church.

WATSON – A crazed American woman out the pages of history crosses an ocean with a fake diary on a quest for revenge after she's visited by some unknown stranger…whoever the devil he is

HOLMES – Haven't you figured that out by now?

WATSON – No

HOLMES – I'm disappointed in you, old friend…after all these years. There is only one man he possibly *could* be…It's Professor Moriarty

WATSON – Moriarty? He fell to his death eight years ago!

HOLMES – I saw him fall and *assumed* him dead. Watson, there is but one belief I permit myself that cannot be empirically proven…the certainty that I always know when Moriarty is the author of a deed. And I tell you, Moriarty is the author of *this* deed.

WATSON – Moriarty still alive…unimaginable

HOLMES – I know that man's evil signature. I can sense his presence the way a jungle animal can sense the presence of a predator. It's an ability I've had since I was a boy. *(He pauses for a long moment)* when Moriarty was my mathematics tutor

WATSON – *(After a pause)* What are you saying?

HOLMES – It was Moriarty who dishonored my mother and caused her death

WATSON – *(Incredulous)* My God…. then *that* is why…you have…

HOLMES – Chased him across all these years… I suppose I want vengeance no less than the poor deluded Mrs. Tonry.

WATSON – *(After a pause)* What do you suppose Moriarty's motive is?

HOLMES – Somehow, he became aware of Reverend Corbett's whereabouts and Mrs. Tonry's…life's work. He created the false diary and gave it to her along with the information about me knowing it would provide her with the perfect reason, opportunity and cover for taking her revenge.

WATSON – But why?

HOLMES – I do not know. To force me *out* of retirement or to shame my legacy *in* retirement…or both?

WATSON – He could have shamed you at any time in the past. Why didn't he do it?

HOLMES – Revealing my father's murder of my mother would have revealed his own adulterous behavior. It has always amused me that the most heinous criminals guard the appearance of social respectability so fiercely.

WATSON – Why was he willing to risk being revealed now? He must have known you would not submit to blackmail

HOLMES – Perhaps he no longer cares about appearing respectable. As to my relationship to Booth, I've always wondered why he didn't make it public. Perhaps he was waiting for the time it would do me the most harm…or him the most good.

WATSON – And he invested such effort in that false history he created. It certainly fooled Mrs. Tonry. But to what end? Did he want Reverend Corbett dead as well?

HOLMES – Not so fast Watson

WATSON – What do you mean?

HOLMES – I said the diary was a fake because it was forged. That does not necessarily mean the story it told was false

WATSON – But you refuted it

HOLMES – Because I was *able* to. The true and final history of the Lincoln assassination has yet to be written. Most of the files relating to it are still American state secrets.

WATSON – Do you think the conspiracy is real?

HOLMES – I do not know what to think

A young woman, Loveday Brooke steps abruptly into Holmes and Watson's path

LOVEDAY – *(Breathless)* Sherlock Holmes…Mr. Holmes…Dr. Watson! I'm so glad to have found you. I was on my way to your flat and…

HOLMES – *(Cutting her off, speaks to Watson)* I blame you for this Watson. The illustrations that accompany your magazine tales are too lifelike. *(To Loveday)* While I am flattered by your enthusiasm young lady my associate and I are engaged in serious business at the moment

LOVEDAY – As I am.

WATSON – What are you saying?

LOVEDAY – I am not merely and enthusiastic young lady Mr. Holmes and I am *not* an avid reader of your stories Dr. Watson. In fact, it often occurs to me that popular detective stories, for which there seems too large a demand at present, must be, at times, uncommonly useful to the criminal classes.

HOLMES – Ah, a young lady with a trifle of good sense. I've been attempting to explain this to my colleague here for years.

LOVEDAY – Your compliment is duly noted, Mr. Holmes…but I wish to tell you…

WATSON – *(Cutting her off)* Please excuse us. We have had quite a day…and I fear it is not so much as half finished.

HOLMES – Indeed…And whatever business you imagine you have with me I am most decidedly *not* accepting any new cases at this time.

LOVEDAY – I am not offering you a case. I'm delivering a message

WATSON – A message?

LOVEDAY – It's a warning from my employer Ebenezer Dyer

HOLMES – You are employed by Ebenezer Dyer?

LOVEDAY – Well…Let us just say I am endeavoring to prove myself to him.

WATSON – As a maid?

LOVEDAY – As a detective

WATSON – A detective? Incredible!

HOLMES – After what we just learned of Mrs. Hughes nothing surprises me

LOVEDAY – Mr. Dyer gave me the assignment of locating you as quickly as possible and…here I am.

WATSON – Who is Ebenezer Dyer?

HOLMES – He is the chief of an investigative agency in Lynch Court. If memory serves their office is to be found on Fleet Street. *(To Loveday)* And you are?

LOVEDAY – My name is Loveday Brooke

HOLMES – Now, Miss Brooke, tell me very clearly and
concisely what warning you have for me, and we shall be on
our way.

LOVEDAY – Do you know of a man by the name of Luigi
Lucheni?

HOLMES – The assassin? *(Watson looks puzzled)* He
stabbed the Austrian Empress, Elizabeth to death one year
ago.

LOVEDAY – He has been in Geneva's Évêché prison ever
since

WATSON – He was not hanged?

HOLMES – No…much to his chagrin capital punishment has
been abolished in Switzerland

WATSON – Much to his chagrin?

HOLMES – Lucheni is anarchist Watson. He wanted to be
martyred for the cause. What does Lucheini have to do with me?

LOVEDAY – He was writing his memoir in prison but it was
stolen and thought destroyed

HOLMES – What a loss for world literature

LOVEDAY – But it was *not* destroyed…It was delivered to the
agency this very morning.

HOLMES – Fascinating…Who delivered it?

LOVEDAY – We do not know, Mr. Holmes. He would not provide his name. From what Mr. Dyer told me, he simply handed him the pages and said, "Mr. Sherlock Holmes should know of this." When Mr. Dyer attempted to question him, he fled. My employer then assigned me the task of finding you.

WATSON – Precisely like Mrs. Tonry's mysterious visitor. *(To Holmes)* Do you think it was...

HOLMES – *(Cutting him off)* There is nothing more deceptive than the obvious Watson. *(To Loveday)* What did your visitor want me to know?

LOVEDAY – Lucheni wrote about you...A circle was drawn around the paragraph and each word was underlined. He called you a mortal enemy of the people who has been targeted for death.

WATSON – Disturbing...but an idle threat from a man in prison

HOLMES – Lucheni and his ilk do not make idle threats. *(To Loveday)* Thank you Miss Brooke. Please convey my regards to Mr. Dyer.

LOVEDAY – I shall. Oh, and please accept my apology for accosting you in the street. It is not my practice to chase after men, regardless of their reputation.

HOLMES – No apology necessary. You fulfilled your assignment admirably.

LOVEDAY – Thank you....*(She turns to leave but turns back)* It was an honor to meet both of you.

Loveday Exits

WATSON – Do you take this threat seriously?

HOLMES – I do…until I have reason not to

WATSON – Do you think that paragraph is genuine or a forgery like Booth's diary pages?

HOLMES – That does not matter. *(Abruptly changing the subject)* Watson, what did you tell Reverend Corbett about me?

WATSON – Nothing. As you requested, I did not even mention your name

HOLMES – What do you think he meant when he asked me not to put my cross down?

WATSON – It does not matter what *I* think he meant. What do *you* think?

HOLMES – There is a reason Her Majesty has protected Reverend Corbett all these years…There is a reason an anarchist's alleged ravings were delivered to Ebenezer Dyer. Moriarty is involved in this…but how…and why?

WATSON – What are you saying Holmes?

HOLMES – Life is stranger than anything which the mind of man could invent.

WATSON – What does that mean?

HOLMES – It means, old friend that the game is still very much afoot!

Outside 221B Baker Street

The Present

MARY – What a story. The women in your family certainly were fertile.

IRENE – What?

MARY – Had fertile *imaginations* I mean

ELLEN – That they did. Well Irene, thank you for the...entertaining tale. Now that it's over, if you don't mind, I'm cold and I'm hungry and I see a cozy pub there on the corner that's calling my name.

IRENE – I don't mind...but it's not over

ELLEN – There's more?

IRENE – I haven't even gotten to the good part yet

MARY – Tell me...tell me

ELLEN – Can I at least sit down?

IRENE –Two years passed. A new century had begun. Another American president, William McKinley took an assassin's bullet. As he fought for his life, Holmes was about to receive an unexpected...but often longed for...visitor

77

The street outside the residence

September 9th 1901

Holmes, looking haggard and tired is walking briskly toward the residence when he sees the Repent Woman

REPENT WOMAN – Repent! Repent! The end is near! Repent while there is still time

Holmes attempts to avoid her but she steps in front of him

REPENT WOMAN – *(To Holmes)* Only you can save them!

Holmes pushes her aside and practically runs away from her

Later that night in Holmes' bedroom

It is dark, save for the flickering glow of a gaslight on the street coming through the window and shining on Holme's sleeping figure. A dark shape passes by the window, momentarily blocking the light. Holmes' eyes snap open.

HOLMES – Who is it...who's there?

IRENE ADLER – *(From the shadows)* No one you need fear

HOLMES – *(Grabbing a pistol from the night table)* Who are you?

IRENE ADLER – Could you have forgotten the sound of my voice?

HOLMES – *(After a moment)* Irene? Pardon me...I mean Mrs. Norton...How did you...?

IRENE ADLER – *(Cutting him off)* Mrs. Hudson...let me in. But please do not be cross with her. I may have...led her to believe... that you were expecting me...She was quite intrigued by the idea

HOLMES – I'm sure. Have you and your husband returned to London?

IRENE ADLER – No...Godfrey will never come back here. He fears you too much

HOLMES – Fears me?

IRENE ADLER – You and King Wilhelm

HOLMES – That blackmail business about the photograph of you and the king?

IRENE ADLER – I never understood all that fuss over a little picture of a future king and a simple, innocent American girl from New Jersey

HOLMES – There is nothing simple or innocent about you…and in any event that was years ago

IRENE ADLER – I *did* leave you a photograph to return to the king

HOLMES – Not the one he sought

IRENE ADLER – No…but I thought it a nice likeness. I hope his majesty was pleased

HOLMES – He was pleased that you kept your word and never revealed the photograph of the two of you. He never saw the one of you alone that you left

IRENE ADLER – No?

HOLMES – I kept it for myself

IRENE ADLER – I see

HOLMES – A remembrance of the only woman who ever bested me

IRENE ADLER – I never thought of it that way. Being suspected of blackmail made me feel dirty and cheap.

HOLMES – *(After a moment)* Why have you come?

IRENE ADLER – To give you this for one thing *(She takes a small, framed photograph from her handbag and hands it to Holmes)*

HOLMES – The famous picture of you and Wilhelm….why now?

IRENE ADLER – I thought you might like to have it…I will miss it though…and not because of that silly old blowhard Wilhelm…without that picture we never would have met

HOLMES – *(Softly)* I would treasure it for the same reason. *(Handing the picture back to her)* but… you keep it for now…as a remembrance of me

IRENE ADLER – As you wish

HOLMES – What is the real reason you are here?

IRENE ADLER – I'm afraid for my husband

HOLMES – Why?

IRENE ADLER – He has gotten himself involved in something sinister….and I do not think he knows how to get out of it.

HOLMES – Tell me more

IRENE ADLER – I do not know much more to tell. He took on a new client some months ago that has taken over his life

HOLMES – Who is this client?

IRENE ADLER – I do not know and Godfrey will not tell me. He says it is to protect me. All I know is this client requires him to work at all hours… to frequent the kinds of places Godfrey would never dream of going to on his own. And he is always afraid. He tries to hide it from me but I know. If this goes on much longer it would not surprise me if he took his own life.

HOLMES – How can I help?

IRENE ADLER – I know I have no right to ask this of you …but are the only man I know who can discover what is going on and stop it before it is too late.

HOLMES – *(After a long pause)* I will do what I can. You have my word

IRENE ADLER – *(Tearfully)* Thank you. *(She kisses him)*

Later that day at the entryway to 221 B. Watson is at the door.

MRS. HUDSON – Doctor Watson! It is good to see you again sir!

WATSON – It is good to see you again as well. I've missed you, Mrs. Hudson

MRS. HUDSON – And we have missed *you* sir

WATSON – I don't doubt that *you* have missed me. Are you sure the same is true of your lodger?

MRS. HUDSON – Don't be silly! He sent for you, didn't he? *(She leans in and whispers)* And maybe you can help him get back to normal again

WATSON – What do you mean?

MRS. HUDSON – The flat is a mess. He's a mess. And the parade of women in and out of here! It's like nothing I've ever seen

WATSON – Parade of women?

HOLMES – Mrs. Hudson? Who is at the door

MRS. HUDSON – Dr. Watson is here to see you sir

HOLMES – Send him in

Watson enters

WATSON – Holmes!

HOLMES – You're late

WATSON – *(Sarcastically)* I am well. Thank you for asking

HOLMES – I am glad you are well…but you are still late

WATSON – I am sorry. I was at a society meeting and it lasted longer than I anticipated

HOLMES – Society meeting?

WATSON – The Fabian Society

HOLMES – I see you are still not cured of your belief in Utopian nonsense

WATSON – *(Wearily)* The Fabian Society does *not* promote Utopian nonsense as you call it. *(He looks around the room)* I see you have not yet chosen to employ the services of a competent maid

HOLMES – I cannot afford a maid, competent or otherwise. Since you chose to pursue a life of wedded bliss…once again… I am fortunate to have funds sufficient to pay Mrs. Hudson the rent…how many wives does this make? And at your age!

WATSON – *(Ignores the question)* What about retirement and your bees?

HOLMES – I have no time for that now

WATSON – Are you not taking cases?

HOLMES – I have a case

WATSON – I mean *paying* cases

HOLMES – I have no time for them either. Besides the case I'm working on has certain…compensations

WATSON – Holmes, your obsession with this conspiracy will be the death of you. It has been two years. Do you even have any proof that Moriarty is alive?

HOLMES – No

WATSON – Have you discovered a reason for the Crown's protection of Corbett?

HOLMES – No

WATSON – Or the alleged warning from the anarchist assassin?

HOLMES – No

WATSON – Give it up man!

HOLMES – I will not give it up now when it seems that events are moving my investigation to a climactic moment

WATSON – What events?

HOLMES – *(Holding up the newspaper)* Have you not heard the news from America?

WATSON – Yes…bad business. Does McKinley still live?

HOLMES – They say his condition is improving

WATSON – I cannot see how…a wound through the stomach is nearly always fatal

HOLMES – Perhaps you are too gloomy a diagnostician. I hear that Mrs. Tonry still lives…happily and quietly reunited with her family in Baltimore.

WATSON – A kidney disorder and a gunshot wound to a vital organ are two very different things

HOLMES – Why no charges were brought against her I *still* cannot say

WATSON – How does the shooting of the American president move your investigation to a climactic moment?

HOLMES – *(Pacing)* McKinley is the third American president to be shot. Each shooting happened on a Friday by the way.

WATSON – Is that significant?

HOLMES – No, just a coincidence. But now *(He shakes the newspaper)* a larger conspiracy is found!

WATSON – What are you talking about?

HOLMES – McKinley's shooter, Leon Czolgosz has admitted to acting at the behest of Emma Goldman and an international anarchist conspiracy. Goldman has been arrested along with nine others. *(Watson takes the paper)* They're being held in America...in Chicago. *(Pauses)* It may interest you to know that she describes herself as a Fabian Society socialist.

WATSON – That's preposterous

HOLMES – Her words. Apparently, your little band is more than an odd array of starry eyed idealists who believe in the myth of human perfectibility

WATSON – We are not starry eyed...and we do *not* believe in political violence

HOLMES – The anarchists do

WATSON – We are not anarchists!

HOLMES – But this Goldman woman...the high priestess of anarchists... says *she* is a Fabian. Forgive me Watson but I am confused

WATSON – Did you send for me to argue politics? If so, please do not waste my time or yours. I am as well aware of your views as you are of mine. I do not think there is much chance of either one of us changing our minds

HOLMES – I sent for you because I need your help

WATSON – With what?

The doorbell rings

HOLMES – If you had been on time, I would have been able to tell you

Madeline enters

MADELINE – Dr. Watson. It's a pleasure to see you again

WATSON – The...*unexpected* pleasure is mine Mrs. Hughes

MADELINE – On behalf of the Crown, I thank you for your help

WATSON – On behalf of the...Holmes, what goes on here?

HOLMES – I have not yet had an opportunity to formally *ask* Watson for his help

MADELINE – Oh...my apologies

WATSON – None are necessary...from *you* Madame. Tell me, how is the Reverend?

MADELINE – You have not heard?

WATSON – Heard what?

MADELINE – *(After a pause)* The Reverend passed away six months ago

WATSON – I am truly sorry to hear that

MADELINE – His end was peaceful

HOLMES – He asked about you often

WATSON – How do you know that?

HOLMES – I visited him frequently…especially in his last months

WATSON – I see…

HOLMES – *(To Madeline)* My friend is a married man now

MADELINE – *(To Watson)* Congratulations

WATSON – Thank you

HOLMES – We have seen very little of each other recently

WATSON – *(To Madeline)* You are still employed by The Crown then?

MADELINE – After the Reverend's death I was given a new assignment, working with Sherlock

WATSON – *(To Holmes)* I thought you were working exclusively on *your* case *(He does a double take)*…Sherlock?

HOLMES – I still am. Madeline, would you be kind enough to explain things for Watson's benefit?

WATSON – *(Another double take)* Madeline?

MADELINE – Certainly. A network of violent radicals is assassinating world leaders. The Spanish Prime Minister and the King of Italy were shot dead. The French President and

Austria Hungary's Empress were stabbed to death. Now the American President has been assaulted and we have reason to believe that King Edward is next

During the ensuing dialogue Madeline busies herself trying to tidy up

WATSON – What is your assignment?

HOLMES – His majesty has requested that I sail for America at once. My plan is to interview Emma Goldman and infiltrate the anarchists imprisoned with her

WATSON – Infiltrate them? How?

HOLMES – Through you…and Miss Brooke

WATSON – Miss Brooke?

HOLMES – You met her briefly two years ago

WATSON – Oh yes…the young lady.

HOLMES – She has become quite the accomplished detective. Disguises are her specialty.

WATSON – She is working with you as well?

HOLMES – She is…on loan from Ebenezer Dyer

WATSON – Why me?

HOLMES – Because you have a better understanding of these people than I do. Besides, the risk of my being recognized is too great

WATSON – And the risk to me is not?

HOLMES – The chances of *your* being recognized are very slim

WATSON – That's not what I meant. And how do *I* have a better understanding of *these* people, as you call them?

HOLMES – You're a socialist, aren't you?

WATSON – Well…yes but I'm not an anarchist

HOLMES – Apparently, in their minds there is very little difference

WATSON – You are asking me to become a spy

HOLMES – Yes

WATSON – Against people whose goals I share even if I deplore their tactics

HOLMES – I am asking you to do it for your King and country

WATSON – *(After a long pause)* I…am not sure I can do that again

HOLMES – *(Taking Madeline aside)* I need to have a private word with my associate if you don't mind

MADELINE – Of course. *(She takes an envelope from her bag)* Here are two first class tickets on the Celtic. She sails tomorrow from Liverpool. And two private compartments have been reserved for you and Dr. Watson on a train from New York to Chicago. We should arrive there by Friday the 20th

WATSON – We?

MADELINE – Miss Brooke and I will be accompanying the two of you

HOLMES– *(Looking at Watson)* If there *are* two of us. Thank you, Madeline… I'll see you out

MADELINE – *(As she and Holmes exit)* I hope to see you on board Doctor

WATSON – Good day Madame

Madeline and Holmes exit. Watson paces, lost in thought. After a moment, Holmes re-enters. Watson continues pacing, saying nothing

HOLMES – *(After watching Watson for a moment)* Come on Watson….out with it

WATSON – *(Seething)* Out with what?

HOLMES – Out with whatever is boiling over in that brain of yours

WATSON – You are the most arrogant, presumptuous, self-righteous…. *(He searches for another word)*

HOLMES – Dictatorial?

WATSON – Dictatorial man I have ever known! When you volunteered me for this mission did you, for one moment stop to consider my wife's welfare…not to mention mine? Did you even briefly reflect on my beliefs and convictions?

HOLMES – Oh please! Spare me another recitation of your beliefs and convictions! And as to your welfare, I hardly think it safe for you or your lovely Mary to live in a country with assassins roaming about

WATSON – If there *are* assassins roaming about, their targets do not include us

HOLMES – What are you saying?

WATSON – I'm saying that I no longer consider the monarch's life more valuable than my own

HOLMES – What happened to your commitment to honor?

WATSON – My honor now serves another master

HOLMES – The commune?

Watson and Holmes circle each other like jungle cats

WATSON – Despite the condescending sneer that always accompanies the word when *you* say it…yes.

HOLMES – I will never understand how your unending *spiritual* quest led you to *atheist* socialism

WATSON – Then I will explain it…again! The people's leaders betray them. Industrialists exploit them. The church stifles the human spirit. The poor have no protector…all under the approving eye of Parliament and The Crown. The established government has no more right to call itself my ruler than the smoke of London has to call itself the weather

HOLMES – So you would sweep away all the institutions of western civilization and replace them with what?

WATSON – With pragmatic solutions

HOLMES – Based on?

WATSON – Whatever works!

HOLMES – The ends justify the means then?

WATSON – If the means include violence, no. But any peaceful means that eliminate private property and puts the machinery of production in the hands of the people, yes

HOLMES – You are advocating theft

WATSON – I am advocating stealing from thieves to create a compassionate society

HOLMES – And what principles will this compassionate society be based upon?

WATSON – Compassion *is* a principle

HOLMES – No, it's an emotion!

WATSON – And we both know how you feel about those

HOLMES – You have no idea

WATSON – Clearly!

HOLMES – Will compassion tell you how to run this new society? Will you help people by giving them money? Whose money? Money stolen from those you deem to have too much? What happens when that money is gone? Making the needs of some an automatic claim on the rights and property of others is oppression not compassion!

WATSON – I can no longer pretend to be blind to societies problems

HOLMES – I see the same problems but the solutions you advocate will become ever greater problems

WATSON – What is *your* solution?

HOLMES – Making the institutions you would destroy live up to their own ideals. They are imperfect because they are run by fallible, self-interested human beings. The utopia you envision will be run by the same people

WATSON – WE WILL RISE ABOVE SELF INTEREST!

HOLMES – *(Quietly)* Perhaps *some* will. But for others your communal bliss will be a stifling tyranny

They both sit...exhausted

WATSON – *(after a pause)* I am sorry I raised my voice Holmes

HOLMES – I know I am asking more from you than I ever have in the past. And I will understand if you decline

WATSON – *(With a sigh, after a long pause)* What is the purpose of this infiltration?

HOLMES – To determine if the nine men imprisoned along with Miss Goldman are in fact part of an organized network and to learn what their plans may be

WATSON – Can't you learn that by questioning Miss Goldman?

HOLMES – I won't learn anything of value by questioning her. She's never cooperated with any law enforcement authority. I doubt she'll make an exception for me.

WATSON – Then why interview her?

HOLMES – Are you familiar with the American card game of poker?

WATSON – I have heard of it, yes

HOLMES – Bluffing... purposely misleading your opponent about the strength of your hand...is one of the game's more fascinating strategies

WATSON – What are you getting at?

HOLMES – I plan to bluff Miss Goldman…and Moriarty

WATSON – How?

HOLMES – I will tell Miss Goldman that I know all about the conspiracy and it's mastermind. I am wagering that her response, even if she lies, will tell me all I need to know. As for Moriarty I have circulated a rumor within the underworld that I am going to America because she has identified *him* as the mastermind behind the attack on President McKinley and the recent assassinations in Europe

WATSON – To what end?

HOLMES – To draw him into the light…and to America

WATSON – Will he believe this…bluff of yours?

HOLMES – Any doubts he may have will be overcome by his fear of exposure… and by his curiosity

WATSON – What about the imprisoned men I am supposed to infiltrate? What makes you think they will accept me? Anarchists have been spied upon by governments for years. They are very suspicious of strangers

HOLMES – A second bluff should assure your acceptance.

WATSON – Second bluff?

HOLMES – Mrs. Hughes has seen to it that immediately after we sail the newspapers will be told that you have denounced The Crown and been exiled from the country. By the time we arrive the inmates will be well aware of the story. You can tell them you came to Chicago to lend them moral support and that you were arrested as soon as you got off the train. After that all you have to do is convince them that you now embrace *their* violent means to achieving the ends you already publicly support

WATSON – What is Miss Brooke's role in all this?

HOLMES – In another newspaper story being arranged by Mrs. Hughes she will be accused… under her assumed identity of an American expatriate…of publicly threatening the life of the King. As a consequence of which she will be deported. Once she gets to Chicago, she'll use the same cover story about being arrested and she will be placed in a cell adjacent to Miss Goldman's

WATSON – And if I do *not* accompany you on this mission?

HOLMES – If my first bluff doesn't work, I will have no way of determining the truth. American authorities have no proof of direct involvement in the assassination on the part of anyone they are holding. Without that proof they will have no choice but to release them and the killings will continue. Meanwhile, I will have to confront Moriarty with no way of putting him behind bars. I will have poked the hornets' nest with no protection…and to no good end

After a long moment Watson begins to exit

HOLMES – Where are you going?

WATSON – Home to pack and convince my wife I am not being deported…or going insane

HOLMES – You do not have to take this risk

WATSON – I have my reasons

Watson exits

An interrogation room at the women's annex of Harrison Street Jail, Chicago Illinois.

September 20th, 1901

Madeline is seated at a table. After a moment Holmes enters

HOLMES – Has the prisoner been sent for?

MADELINE – She is on her way now.

HOLMES – We are fortunate she and her associates are still here.

MADELINE – We are. Even though the charges became conspiracy to murder when McKinley died there is still no proof of their involvement.

HOLMES – Has Watson met the nine men?

MADELINE – His cell is adjacent to theirs. The guards tell me they've been talking

HOLMES – Good…and Miss Brooke?

MADELINE – Miss Goldman has been proselytizing her since she arrived

HOLMES – The poor girl. How is she holding up?

MADELINE – She's playing the role of the wide eyed, young devotee masterfully.

Emma Goldman enters, handcuffed and escorted by an armed guard who shows her to a seat at the table and stands in the shadows

EMMA – *(Looks at Holmes with recognition and surprise)* Are you the next interrogators to put me through the third degree?

HOLMES – You are Miss Goldman I presume?

EMMA – I am.

HOLMES – The photographs of you in the press do not do you justice

EMMA – Flattery from the great Sherlock Holmes. Is this how you soften up your female victims?

HOLMES – You know who I am?

EMMA – Of course. They must be truly desperate to have brought *you* here. But don't flatter yourself. To me you are just another state lackey. I suppose you want me to tell my story again

HOLMES – Not particularly *(Emma looks dumbfounded)*

MADELINE – *I* would like to hear your story

EMMA – A female interrogator?

MADELINE – I am an agent of the Crown

EMMA – Could the corrupt British bourgeois be that progressive?

MADELINE – I am educated and well qualified for the work I do

HOLMES – Get on with it please, Madam

EMMA – As you wish…. When Czolgosz was questioned about his propaganda of the deed he…

HOLMES – *(Cutting her off)* Propaganda of the deed?

EMMA – His shooting of this man McKinley was a decisive political action taken to radicalize the masses and hasten the onset of the revolution. Ideas spring from deeds Mr. Holmes, not the other way around

HOLMES – I see

EMMA – During his interrogation Czolgosz said he was inspired to act after hearing me speak. The authorities used that as an excuse to charge me with planning the assassination. They tracked me to the home of friends in Chicago and arrested me along with nine innocent comrades

MADELINE – And you had no previous acquaintance with the assassin?

EMMA – Once, during a talk I gave in Cleveland, he approached me to ask which books he should read. He asked… *unusual* questions. I assumed he was an infiltrator like all the others sent to spy on me. But apparently, I was wrong. He is a true revolutionary.

MADELINE – Why do you say that?

EMMA – He has struck terror in the enemy's ranks and made them realize that the proletariat of America has its avengers

HOLMES – Was this proletariat asking to be avenged? I see no outpouring of gratitude from them

EMMA – As a revolutionary he expects none. The deluded masses mourn McKinley but none will mourn Comrade Czolgosz after he is murdered for the crime of being sensitive to their pain and doing something to ease it. Now...I have told you my story. I will answer no more questions

HOLMES – Good. I have none to ask

EMMA – Why did you wish to see me then?

HOLMES – To bring you a message from your superior

EMMA – My what?

HOLMES – Professor James Moriarty

GUARD – How thoughtful of you to carry messages for me

The guard turns around slowly, revealing himself to be Moriarty

HOLMES – Moriarty?

MORIARTY – You're slipping Holmes. You didn't recognize me standing in the same room with you. Maybe it really *is* time for you to retire. But…in fairness being pushed over the edge of a cliff did somewhat alter my appearance. *(Smiling)* I have you to thank for that.You did get one thing right though. I *am* her superior…I am *everyone's* superior… But Miss Goldman and I are not acquainted so I cannot imagine what message you have for her

HOLMES – How the devil did you get in here?

MORIARTY – I am a welcome guest anywhere in the fair city of Chicago. And it's such a bargain too. The politicians and police are cheap here. Are you surprised I did not die from my fall Holmes?

HOLMES – No…I knew you were still alive

MORIARTY – Miss Goldman, there are vicious rumors circulating that you have accused me of high crimes

EMMA – What are you talking about? Who are you?

MORIARTY – Where are my manners? *(He grabs Emma by the neck and leans into her)* I am James Moriarty…Professor James Moriarty. Perhaps you've read some of my mathematical studies…

EMMA – *(Frightened)* No

MORIARTY – Brilliant work if I do say so myself…but no, I suppose you wouldn't have read them. Marx is more your cup of tea. *(He releases Emma and turns to Madeline)* And while *we* have not been formally introduced, Mrs. Hughes, I *did* have the pleasure of meeting your late husband *(He hands Madeline a photograph of her husband's corpse)*

MADELINE – *(In shock)* William?

MORIARTY – Yes…four years ago it was. But sadly, the occasion of our meeting was most unpleasant for him

MADELINE – Four years ago? You… *you*…killed my husband? Why? *(She pulls out a pistol and points it at Moriarty)*

MORIARTY – Because I could. And please spare us all the ordeal of avenging him by shooting me. We're all armed…but it seems the guards in this jail are all on my side

HOLMES – You did not come here to torment Mrs. Hughes. You came for me so let's finish this game

MORIARTY – Marvelous idea! I completely agree. At our age it is time to finally be finished with games. But there is someone missing

HOLMES – What? Who?

MORIARTY – Someone very important to our…game. *(Calling off camera)* Gentlemen? Could you please show the prisoner in?

Watson, a bag over his head and bound by a rope is dragged into the room by a guard and pushed down in a chair. An explosive device with red and black wires is strapped to his chest. The guard places the detonator on his lap.

WATSON – I…am…sorry Holmes. Please forgive me

HOLMES – *(Removing the bag from Watson's head)*
Watson!

MORIARTY – And you have much to forgive the Doctor
for, Mr. Holmes

WATSON – I had no idea this would happen

MORIARTY – How could you? Nothing is what it seems
these days…and no *one*. It's hard to know what to believe
with so many tall tales being bandied about. Of course, the
Doctor never even *told* his tall tale

HOLMES – *(To Watson)* What happened?

MORIARTY – And what a tale it was! Exiled! On a
pilgrimage of solidarity…he didn't say any of that. No, this
idiot told the truth!

WATSON – I thought…I thought…

MORIARTY – You thought your brothers in arms would
understand what a good heart you have…how pure your
intentions are

HOLMES – *(Angrily)* DAMNIT!

MORIARTY – You all want the same things after all! The
workers' paradise! *(He approaches Holmes)* The eternal
idyll! *(Holmes pushes him away)* Your comrades would
never betray *you*…the way you betrayed Holmes!

WATSON – No!

MORIARTY – When it's a contest between your politics and your friend… we know which one wins. The Doctor had barely crossed the threshold of his cell when he spilled his guts…just couldn't bring himself to be a bourgeois tool in the service of the evil state. You underestimated your friend's commitment to the cause and overestimated his friendship for *you* Mr. Holmes. Not that *your* hands are clean. Your lie about Miss Goldman brought me here. And as soon as I arrived, I paid a call on my anarchist friends in this jail who told me the whole nasty business

HOLMES – So you *are* part of the conspiracy!

MORIARTY – There *is* no conspiracy! At least not the one you've been chasing. We all crave easy explanations and final solutions. This fanciful notion of an internationally coordinated conspiracy is something you have created in the theater of your mind. Ours is a world of slippery truths Holmes. Succeeding in it requires the manipulation of perception…and I am a master at that. But one truth that is *not* slippery is that the gentlemen unjustly imprisoned here are not conspirators. They are my customers

HOLMES – Customers?

MORIARTY – *(Gesturing to the device strapped to Watson)* This is one of my best-selling products. *(He picks up the detonator)* I can't wait to show you how it works

HOLMES – Are you mad?

MORIARTY – Is that a rhetorical question? No…I suppose not. I have my occasional moments of lunacy…as you do. And speaking of *your* lunacy, before you judge the Doctor for what he's done to you, consider what you've done to him. Your obsession with revenge against me has finally driven you mad. In the end…and this *is* the end… it will drive you to take your friend's life...and Miss Goldman's…and the nine men in the cells below us…and mine. *(He hands the detonator to Holmes)* It's a mighty powerful bomb. Mrs. Hughes will die as well of course but I think she's lost her zest for life since her husband's death.*(He approaches Madeline and looks at her for a long moment…He then abruptly turns his head and looks at Holmes)* Or perhaps she's found it again. What say you Holmes?

MADELINE – Bastard…

MORIARTY – Actually I'm not…but I've sired a few

HOLMES – What are you doing Moriarty?

MORIARTY – I should think it would be perfectly clear. I am bringing our game to a conclusion…and I am letting *you* win! You accomplish your life's goal…avenging your mother's honor by killing me. You end the life of your duplicitous former friend, which despite any regret you may feel does the world a favor by ridding it of one more socialist. And at the same time, you eliminate the queen of anarchy and nine of her most vicious apostles. Not a final victory perhaps but a real blow for King and country

EMMA – You *are* mad!

MORIARTY – What's wrong Miss Goldman? Is becoming a martyr for the cause more than you bargained for?

HOLMES – What's in this for you Moriarty? What do you gain from your own death?

MORIARTY – A small measure of immortality. Just as *your* purpose in life has been to destroy me, my only real purpose has been to control

HOLMES – Control what?

MORIARTY – Everything! People, money, life…death. But with advancing years I came to realize that control does not create a legacy…in fact, quite the opposite. When I am gone all I will leave is my absence. But, if through my final act I engineer the death of the woman whose ideas will change the world for good or ill. Well… let's just say we'll both be immortalized in the pages of history books… *(To Watson)* not just in the pulp pages of penny dreadfuls

HOLMES – Then it *was* you who sent Mrs. Tonry

MORIARTY – I didn't even *try* to hide that

HOLMES – Why?

MORIARTY – To see if *your* need to be remembered was as strong as mine. I think I got my answer

HOLMES – Was there any truth in the diary pages you convinced her were written by Booth?

MORIARTY – Yes…and no. That was the fun of it! I think I have a real flair for historical fiction…I now give you all the opportunity to pose for posterity! *(He arranges everyone in a pose)* Guard! Bring me the camera! *(A guard scurries in and hands Moriarty a box camera)* Now…look forward radiant angels with bleeding wings…smile! *(He presses the shutter)*

A few of the Queen's ministers and some men heavily invested in cotton were not as neutral as she was during the…unpleasantness… between the American states.

(He re-arranges their poses) Here, the mighty Holmes, mentee to Dr. James Moriarty! *(He presses the shutter again)*

Bribing Members of Parliament…. ugly business! Victoria became aware of their little scheme the day after Lincoln was killed. She was afraid of what would happen to her court and the government if the scheme was revealed so royal agents arranged to have Booth killed before he could testify.

Ahh! The revolutionary Emma, inhaling my wisdom *(The shutter sounds again)*

So, you see the late Reverend Corbett was not only the avenger of Lincoln. He was the savior of the Crown. But he was a dangerous savior. What did he know? He acted mad. But was he? Did he believe it was the voice of God that told him to shoot Booth…or did he know the truth.?

(To Madeline) Well, you know the value of a photograph, don't you? *(To Watson)* And Dr. John Watson, the champion of the people! *(He presses the shutter again)*

Once her majesty learned that the conspirators were trying to eliminate Corbett, she protected him…for life. The poor old girl couldn't bring herself to have him killed after he had…inadvertently…served her so well.

HOLMES – Why did *you* try to have him killed by Mrs. Tonry?

MORIARTY – I didn't. Corbett didn't matter to me one way or the other. He was just the bait that attracted the fish… *(He points to Holmes)* that attracted the *bigger* fish

HOLMES – How did you come to know this state secret in the first place?

MORIARTY – When I was a much younger man one of the schemers confided it to me. He was my employer at the time. He had hired me… as a tutor…for his sons *(Holmes is taken aback)* What's the matter Holmes? Not what you were expecting to hear?

WATSON – *(Nervously)* Steady…Holmes

Madeline gets Holmes' attention and gestures toward the detonator with her eyes.

HOLMES – Now…now I understand

MORIARTY – Figuring things out, are you?

HOLMES – Yes

MORIARTY – That's the student I used to know. Your mother would have been so proud. Of course, knowing a state secret is worthless unless you can do something with it. And, oh…. what *I* have done with *this* one! Not only did I use it to bring you out of retirement I used it to blackmail the Crown

MADELINE – What are you saying?

MORIARTY – Edward doesn't want this old, nasty affair tarnishing his mother's legacy. So, I have struck a bargain with him to protect it.

MADELINE – You're extorting money from the King?

MORIARTY – Yes, but not for myself. Thanks to people like Miss Goldman here I now have a social conscience. That is why I am using my…influence … with his majesty to persuade *him* to persuade the kingdom's leading capitalists to support…socialism!

MADELINE – How?

MORIARTY – By funding the Fabian Society

EMMA – The society is a front to spy on us?

MORIARTY – No…those dolts are quite innocent. They really believe all those generous contributions are coming spontaneously from guilt-ridden capitalists.

HOLMES – How is the Crown doing this… persuading?

MORIARTY – Oh...we have one of my best men handling that. A respected barrister...I think you may know him...I believe you may have *known* his wife better.

HOLMES – Godfrey Norton

MORIARTY – Very good Holmes! Perhaps you haven't lost your powers after all

HOLMES – How?

MORIARTY – Mr. Norton's job is to discover the dirty secrets and indiscretions that the rich fear being revealed. They are willing to pay handsomely for their continued concealment

HOLMES – And why would he take on such a job?

MORIARTY – Fear of course. Edward *may* have led him to believe that King Wilhelm still harbors a grudge over some silly old picture of him and his wife. After all, only a king can protect you from a king.

WATSON – Good God!

MORIARTY – Delicious, isn't it? I'm blackmailing The Crown to use the husband of your beloved Irene to blackmail businessmen to support the means of its own eventual destruction

EMMA – You are surely mad, but you strike a blow for the proletariat

MORIARTY – I care nothing for your unwashed proletariat!

WATSON – Why are you doing it then?

MORIARTY – Because I can

HOLMES – Alright Moriarty. You win

MORIARTY – No, *you* win Holmes

WATSON – Holmes! You…you cannot be serious!

HOLMES – *(Holding up the detonator)* This is the only possible move left to play. *(To Moriarty)* Your logic is unassailable. It's a shame we won't live long enough to play a few games of chess. I'm sure I could learn much from you

MORIARTY – As you once did

HOLMES – You *did* teach me logic. *(Fondling the detonator)* Who would have imagined it would end like this?

WATSON – Please…Holmes I am begging you not to do this thing!

EMMA – This taking of life is senseless. It serves no purpose

HOLMES – You only think it's senseless because it does not serve *your* purpose. *(Puts his hand on the plunger)* It makes perfect sense actually. Still, I admit it's sobering to realize how close to the end we are

MORIARTY – Get on with it!

HOLMES – Does anyone have any last words?

MADELINE – I do *(She moves toward Holmes and hold out her hand)* Let me do it

MORIARTY – What? No!

MADELINE – I am ready to die. *(To Moriarty)* All I ask is the pleasure of knowing that you will die by *my* hand

HOLMES – *(Handing the detonator to Madeline)* It is a fair request

MORIARTY – NO! *(He lunges for Madeline, but Holmes restrains him)* THIS IS NOT THE WAY IT'S SUPPOSED TO HAPPEN!

MADELINE – *(To Moriarty, with her hand on the plunger)* Are you ready?

MORIARTY – NO!

MADELINE – Hell…is…waiting…TO RECIEVE YOU!

She pushes the plunger down…

…and nothing happens

WATSON – *(After a long moment, in a shaking voice)* Thank God…

MORIARTY – *(To Madeline in a small, sad voice)* You ruined it…You ruined it

HOLMES – *(Taking the detonator back from Madeline)* Good work

MORIARTY – Good work? What does that mean?

HOLMES – While you were regaling us with your state secrets, Mrs. Hughes caught my eye. She directed my gaze to the wires coming out of your *product* here *(He moves toward Watson)* She had noticed…as I then did…that your bomb was…what's the modern word for it? …a dud

MORIARTY – Dud?

HOLMES – Defective

MORIARTY – Defective?

HOLMES – Anyone with a rudimentary understanding of electricity can see that the grounding wire has become disconnected. When Mrs. Hughes pressed down the plunger no circuit was completed, meaning no spark, meaning no explosion. Mrs. Hughes, your powers of detection are…equal to my own.

MADELINE – *(Surprised and moved)* Thank you

MORIARTY – *(To Madeline)* If you knew this, why were you so insistent on being the one to detonate the bomb

MADELINE – *(With a smile)* Because I could

MORIARTY – I do not understand it…I inspected the detonator…how could the wire have become disconnected.

(The guard who brought Watson into the room removes his hat to reveal a head of long brown hair)

LOVEDAY – I did it

MORIARTY – *(Incredulous)* Who are you?

LOVEDAY – Loveday Brooke

WATSON – *(Equally incredulous)* How did you…? I thought you were impersonating a prisoner locked up with Miss Goldman

EMMA – Another lying pawn of the corrupt bourgeois state!

HOLMES – *(To Watson)* I told you, disguises are her specialty. Masterfully done Miss Brooke.

LOVEDAY – Thank you Mr. Holmes

HOLMES – There's something else you should know Moriarty. My father confided in his *sons* as well as you. He told us about what he did to protect his cotton investments. He wanted Mycroft and I to learn from his mistakes. Of course, my father's biggest mistake was trusting you

MORIARTY – So my exquisitely written diary pages did not surprise you…So sad. The threat of your relationship to Booth being revealed did not intimidate you…so sad. And so sad that our game did not come to a satisfactory conclusion. But I suppose…I suppose life goes on. *(Brightening)* As you said Holmes, who would have imagined it would end like this?

WATSON – How *does* it end?

HOLMES – Not with justice I'm afraid

WATSON – Why not?

MORIARTY – You are not a chess player are you, Doctor?

WATSON – What the devil does that have to do with anything?

HOLMES – We have played to a draw

MORIARTY – Quite right. You or Mrs. Hughes *could* shoot me, but the guards outside would apprehend you both immediately and shoot you on the spot…before shooting the rest of you

EMMA – What about me?

HOLMES – I predict you will be released in a matter of days…along with your friends downstairs. There is no evidence against any of you.

EMMA – I am glad you have finally come to your senses, Mr. Holmes. And I hope someday you will come to your senses about the corrupt bourgeoise you serve

HOLMES – I am in full possession of my senses Madam. And as long as I am I will be the sworn enemy of your ideas and the destruction they cause.

MADELINE – *(To Moriarty)* There is something I want you to know...*Professor*. Even if your bomb wasn't a...dud...I would have gladly set it off for the satisfaction of killing you

MORIARTY – *(With a slight bow)* Until we meet again Madame

MADELINE – And we most assuredly *will* meet again

MORIARTY – *(To Emma)* Oh...Miss Goldman? Your interests and the interests of your cause will be best served by revealing none of what you have witnessed here. Do we understand each other?

EMMA – We do

MADELINE – It's time to get *you* back. Loveday, will you escort your former cellmate?

LOVEDAY – Of course *(She pulls Emma out of her chair. Emma recoils and does her best to shake her off until Loveday finally subdues her)* Let's go...and if you say another word about....about anything...I cannot be held responsible for my actions. *(She starts for the door with Emma but turns back to Watson before she exits)* Dr. Watson...I owe you an apology. When we met, I told you that I was not admirer of your stories...but I lied. I read every one. I would not be here now without them. Perhaps, one day we shall meet again...and work on a case...together *(She and Emma exit. Watson is speechless)*

Madeline starts to follow Loveday and Emma out the door. Before she exits Holmes reaches out and touches her arm

HOLMES – *(Reaching out and touching Madeline's arm)* Madeline?

MADELINE – Yes?

HOLMES – Thank you

MADELINE – *(Placing her hand on his)* You're welcome, Sherlock

Madeline exits

MORIARTY – Well gentlemen it is time for me to take my leave as well

WATSON – Back to England?

MORIARTY – No. I am bored with England. At present, Germany is much better suited to a man of my talents…and Russia. A self-proclaimed mystic priest there has come to my attention. I think we might accomplish great things together. The world order is toppling gentlemen. And if I am to live a while longer, I may as well help it topple.

HOLMES – One more thing Moriarty…In light of events… I request that you relieve Mr. Godfrey of his duties and ask King Edward to assure him that he is safe.

MORIARTY – You never cease to amaze me Holmes

HOLMES – Will you do it then?

Moriarty nods and exits. Holmes helps Watson remove the explosive device

HOLMES – It would appear I will be travelling to Germany and Russia in the near future

WATSON – You're *still* not retiring? Even after all this?

HOLMES – Moriarty was right. The world order *is* toppling. I fear that you and I will live long enough to see very dark times…but not long enough to see them end. And Reverend Corbett was right as well.

WATSON – About what?

HOLMES – It is not yet time for me to put down my cross. I hope you will join me in my travels when you are able

WATSON – Join you?

HOLMES – Even a married man can spare a bit of time to help his friend now and again, can't he?

WATSON – Holmes…I …I don't know what to say. After what I did, I feared I no longer *was* your friend

HOLMES – You acted on your convictions Watson. Misjudging people you thought shared those convictions was not a betrayal. It was a mistake

WATSON – A grave one…and one for which I am truly sorry

HOLMES – I am sorry too, my friend. And *my* mistakes far outnumber yours. I have been ruled by anger and the need for revenge for too long. For whatever future I have left…and whatever that future brings, I choose to be ruled by what Mr. Lincoln called the *better* angels of our nature.

They shake hands

Outside 221B Baker Street, London.

The Present

ELLEN – So…is your tall tale implying that Moriarty was somehow responsible for causing World War One, The Russian revolution and so on and so on?

IRENE – That's the way my mother told it

ELLEN – The women in your family not only had fertile imaginations…they had *grandiose* fertile imaginations

MARY – *(To Irene)* What a shame you won't have a daughter to pass these stories along to…or a son

IRENE – *(Sadly)* Yes….I guess it all ends with me

MARY – Well *I'll* remember your story

IRENE – Thank you

ELLEN – Well, that was a heartwarming moment. But I am still cold. I am still hungry and that pub is still there on the corner. Would you ladies care to join me?

IRENE – You two go ahead. I'll be right behind you.

Mary and Ellen exit.

Irene gazes at the front door to 221B. After glancing in the direction of her friends to be sure they are not watching, she reaches into her coat and takes out the small, framed photograph of Irene Adler and King Wilhelm. She places it

on the front step and turns to go when she is startled to see someone who looks just like…

THE REPENT WOMAN – *(To Irene, smiling)* Only you can save them

IRENE – Who are you?

The Repent Woman hurries away. Irene, clearly shaken takes one last look at the residence and exits.

The End